LEE STRAUSS

Love
Loralee

HEART & SOUL
THE MINSTREL SERIES

aka Lee

HEART & SOUL
by Lee Strauss
Copyright © 2014 Lee Strauss

Cover by Steven Novak Illustration
Formatting by Novel Ninjutsu

ISBN 9781927547267

This is a work of fiction and the views expressed herein are the sole responsibility of the author. Likewise, characters, places and incidents are either the product of the author's imagination or are represented fictitiously and any resemblance to actual persons, living or dead, or actual event or locales, is entirely coincidental.

All rights reserved.

This book, or parts thereof, may not be reproduced in any form without permission.

She's heartbroken. He's heartless.

Gabriele Baumann-Smith is deliriously in love with her young husband Lennon.

Except, it turns out that Lennon Smith isn't his real name. In fact, he's full of secrets: a cottage on the southern British coast, an old girlfriend and... an identical twin brother.

Callum Jones—not his real name—can't believe his brother's widow came to England. He'd warned Mick—Lennon—that an inheritance could put the girl's life in danger, and he was right.

"Mrs. Smith" is the last thing Callum needs to worry about right now. She's beautiful, sure, takes his breath away at times. But when she looks at him, who does she see?

Gabriele's heart is battered and bruised. Can one brother fix what the other left behind? And will they live long enough to find out?

The Minstrel Series books can be read in any order
but are best enjoyed in sequence.
#1 Sun & Moon
#2 Flesh & Bone
#3 Heart & Soul

PERMISSIONS

SUMMERTIME
Words and music by Trisha Robins. Copyright Trisha Robins. Remake recorded by Tasia Strauss. All rights reserved. Used by permission.

HOLES IN THE NIGHT SKY
Words and music by Andrew Smith. Copyright Andrew and Tami Smith. Remake recorded by Tasia Strauss. All rights reserved. Used by permission.

JET STREAM
Words and music by Norm Strauss and Andrew Smith. Copyright Norm Strauss and Andrew Smith. Remake recorded by Tasia Strauss. All rights reserved. Used by permission.

HOPE SO
Words and music by Joshua Smith. Copyright Joshua Smith. Remake recorded by Tasia Strauss. All rights reserved. Used by permission.

CONTENTS

1: Life Goes On 1

2: The Happy Couple 13

3: Foam For My Coffee 18

4: Time and Trouble 23

5: Family Dinner 25

6: Unnecessary But Kind 29

7: That is Crazy Thinking 32

8: No Matter What Happens 38

9: Wrongly Believed 45

10: Something's Wrong 49

11: I Think It's Time 51

12: Blind, Deaf, Drowning 57

13: Nights Are Long 59

14: Valuable and Wasted 62

15: In Light of Us 65

16: Sleep Won't Come 71

17: In Spite of Us 75

18: Wake Me Up in Summertime	....	84
19: Secrets and Scare Tactics	....	87
20: Holes in the Night Sky	....	101
21: Acceptance, Almost	....	108
22: Starlight Swirl	....	113
23: Girls Night	....	118
24: Leave a Light On	....	125
25: The Callahans	....	129
26: A Pretty British Boy	....	136
27: A Kink in the Plan	....	142
28: Above the Wind and Rain	....	151
29: Dew-Covered Grass in the Sun	....	157
30: You Look a Little Uncomfortable	....	166
31: Drink, Drink, Drink	....	171
32: Found	....	175
33: Who Do You Work For, Really?	....	179
34: His Brother's Wife	....	187
35: I Didn't Mean to Hurt You	....	189
36: A Knock on the Door	....	195
37: A Flower at Dusk	....	198

38: Safe and Secure	....	203
39: I'm Not Kissing You Goodbye	....	207
40: The Chase	....	213
41: Something She'd Never Dreamed She'd Do	....	216
42: Gravel Crunching Under Footsteps	....	218
43: Tell Me Something I Don't Know	....	220
44: Ride On a Jet Stream	....	228
45: Fly Like a Kite on a String	....	232
46: High Like a Bird on the Wing	....	240
47: Drift on a Dream	....	247
48: He Came From a Seaside Town	....	251
49: I Gave Him Everything I Had	....	256
50: Why Should I Love You?	....	261
51: Can I Survive This?	....	264
52: I Hope So	....	268
53: Butterfly Kisses	....	272
Sample from Peace & Goodwill, a Christmas Novella	....	
About the Author	....	
Acknowledgments	....	
Song Links	....	

Artist Links ....

Books by Lee Strauss ....

LIFE GOES ON

The flight to London was turbulent and the elderly lady sitting beside Gabriele spent the whole time white-knuckling the hand rests. Gabriele reached over to pat her arm. "It's going to be all right."

The woman smiled through yellow teeth and squinted through watery eyes.

Gabriele smiled back reassuringly, though her heart jumped a little with the next bump.

"Business or pleasure?" the woman asked when the flight had smoothed out. Her accent reminded her of Lennon, and Gabriele had to wrestle down her emotions. Everyone she would meet in England would sound like Lennon. She couldn't break down every time someone spoke.

"Business," she answered.

"I'm just returning home from visiting my grandchildren. My daughter married a German fellow. He's nice enough, though I wish they lived closer. Your family's in Dresden?"

Not long ago Gabriele had said good-bye to her parents at the Dresden airport. Her papa had wrapped her in his customary bear hug and her mama dabbed at tears. The way they went on about her leaving, you'd think she was on her way to America and not just to London, only one hour difference, a time zone away.

Gabriele answered, "My parents and my sister."

The woman's eyes darted to Gabriele's hand. She'd been playing with her wedding ring absentmindedly.

"And a husband?" the woman prodded.

"Oh, no, he's... waiting for me in England." Gabriele didn't know why she said that. She just couldn't bear another bout of pity, especially from a stranger.

"That's nice," the lady said.

Thankfully, the captain announced they would be arriving in London soon. The flight attendants came through and collected the trash and made sure everyone had their seat belts fastened and their chairs in the full upright position. Gabriele hoped she was doing the right thing by coming.

Now she gawked out the window of the black, boxy cab as the driver navigated on the left side of the road. More than once she had to grab her heart when she momentarily forgot they drove on the other side in the United Kingdom, and she believed the approaching traffic was motoring towards them in the same lane.

The cabbie had tried to talk her out of hiring him to take her all the way to Emsworth despite the sign on the inside of the cab that said, "Available for longer journeys."

"That's at least two hours," he said carefully. "That'll cost you a few quid."

Gabriele didn't care. Normally, she was careful with money. Mostly. But now she just needed to see the cottage. Try to find out why Lennon failed to tell her about it. Find out if there was anything else he'd kept from her. Try to find out why he was compelled to keep secrets.

It was a tall order and she knew it. But, even if she went back to Germany without any answers, she hoped to find some kind of closure for her trouble.

Closure. That was the current buzzword. Eva said it. Julia said it. Mama and Papa implied it. Everyone was eager for her to move on and be happy again.

"How long will y'be visitin' England?" the cabbie asked. He was a jolly man who liked to chat, it seemed. Driving all day could be boring, otherwise, Gabriele imagined.

"I'm not sure. A week." Maybe more. Maybe less.

"Yer from Germany? I can hear y'accent."

"Yes. Dresden."

"Ah. I was in Berlin once, back in '89. Wall was still up."

The traffic was heavy as the cabbie directed them through the city along the River Thames. Gabriele strained her gaze out the window, looking for a familiar iconic landmark and was rewarded with a view of the Tower Bridge in the distance. She held her breath. She was really here. In London!

She pulled out her phone and opened the window, captured a shot, then sent it to Eva.

Gabriele Baumann-Smith
I'm here!

Eva Baumann
It looks amazing! Happy for you!!

"Oy, our beautiful Tower Bridge," the cabbie said. "T'was opened a hundred and twenty years ago in 1894. The suspension bridge opens to let tall vessels through. A bloody headache for auto traffic if you're caught in it trying to get to the other side. Looks like we'll be okay today, though."

Gabriele cranked her head up as they drove across. "It's amazing."

"Even lovelier at night all lit up and reflectin' off the river. You'll have to make sure you see it in the evenin' before you go."

The rest of the trip took them through smaller villages and green pastures. Gabriele leaned her head against the glass, staring out as the minutes ticked by. She couldn't help but wonder how many times Lennon had traveled this very road. Her heart squeezed tight. This was her husband's homeland. He should be here with her, giving her the tour. Being here alone was not the fairytale she'd imagined.

She let out a sad sigh.

"You all right, love?" The cabbie glanced at her in his review mirror. "Yer much too pretty a lady to have such a sad expression on yer face."

Gabriele forced a smile at his reflection and then returned

to the pastoral view out the window. There was a patch of blue sky overhead and Gabriele could see the sunlight reflecting off the sea as they grew closer.

The green space ended suddenly as they crossed under the rail tracks and into a neighborhood of small, tightly packed brick houses and then into a snug commercial area.

"This is Emsworth, love," the cabbie said. "Do you have an address?"

Gabriele did. She'd entered it onto the notes app on her phone, but also scribbled it on a piece of paper at the last minute before leaving Dresden, in case something happened to her phone.

The taxi circled around a roundabout and farther into the village in the direction of the English Channel. She knew from studying Google Earth that Emsworth sat on a square-ish peninsula with water along three sides.

The village was quaint and Gabriele could imagine that it looked postcard perfect in the summer. They came to a triangular intersection off High Street, and Gabriele knew the cottage was nearby.

"I can get out here."

"Are you sure, miss?"

"Very." Gabriele had traveled light, only one medium-sized suitcase on wheels and a carry-on that she swung over her shoulder. After traveling all day, she was ready for a walk, and besides, she didn't want a stranger with her when she arrived at the cottage.

She paid the cabbie, careful not to let the shock of the large fee show on her face and then breathed in deeply. She could smell the saline air from the middle of town. It was soothing somehow.

Gabriele pulled her suitcase along the uneven cobblestone surface of the large triangular road divider. It had a little dark wood kiosk with benches attached to the exterior, a decorative lamp post, and a visitor information board. She noted an Indian restaurant and a newspaper outlet along with other small businesses on one side. On the other was a brick building with a sign that said *Methodist Church*. Tucked beside it was The Greenhouse Café surprisingly full for such a small town in off-season. Public access to the sea lay directly south.

Gabriele unfolded the sheet of paper she had tucked into her pocket and studied the map. According to it, she just had to take a right at the next intersection and head straight towards the water.

A pub on the corner had a sign hanging over the door read "Callahan's Irish Pub." Gabriele paused to read a chalkboard sandwich sign situated on the pavement. It listed a schedule for several music events: karaoke, live bands, open mic night. The door opened and a couple walked out, stopping briefly to light cigarettes. Laughter filtered out while the door remained open.

"Wait while I do up my zip," the woman said. "The wind is cold."

Gabriele watched as they walked away in the other direction, towards the town center. The woman linked her arm through the man's and rested her head on his shoulder.

People still played and sang. They still loved and laughed. Life went on.

Gabriele tugged on her suitcase, which felt considerably heavier since she began her trek, and turned the corner.

The street was narrow, hardly wide enough for two cars to pass each other, and was lined with tall brick walls that protected whatever lay on the other side. It ended in a small cul-de-sac. Two roof-lines silhouetted against a smoky-grey, cloud-filled sky. The one on the left was significantly smaller and Gabriele betted that it was the one she was looking for. She double-checked the address and confirmed her assumption. She shivered. This little brick house was hers.

Gabriele pulled her suitcase along the walkway. Long strands of dry grass waved from between the cracks in the red tiles. She removed the envelope from the lawyer from her purse and retrieved the key. It was rusty and she had to fiddle with it, even bumping against the door with her hip to pry it open. The hinges squeaked from lack of use. She was greeted with a waft of stale air. With only the light from the open door, she could hardly make out exactly what was inside.

She left the door open to air out the place. Abandoning her bags, she made a quick sweep of the cottage. The hallway had three closed doors which she didn't take the time to open. Instead, she went directly to the patio doors off the living room that faced the sea and drew the curtains wide. She unbolted the door that led to a terrace. There was a wooden table and a couple matching chairs. A gate on the side of the terrace opened to a set of wooden steps that led to the shore. Everything was wind worn and weather-beaten.

But directly in front of her, a stone's throw away was the sea.

Or at least the seabed. The tide was out and though she could see the glistening water on the horizon, her immediate view looked like a graveyard for old sailboats. To the west a rock wall created a promenade around a manmade pond. It appeared to be a favourite gathering place as a number of people were strolling around it. Gabriele shielded her eyes from the glare of the setting sun. Was that… a swan?

It was. She smiled as she took in the beauty of the large white bird with its long neck looped back so it could tuck its black beak into its wings.

This wasn't the kind of beach that people swarmed to for sunbathing. In fact, it didn't appear to be anything more than a good place to go sailing if she could go by the number of boats tied to buoys in the distance. She leaned over the edge of the rail and stared at the silty seabed below. Crushed shells, pebbles and black moss-like seaweed littered the sand.

Seagulls and other waterfowl chattered overhead. The waves whooshed gently against the shore. Laughter carried from the common area at the foot of the promenade. Broad pink streaks formed in the sky as the sun began to set.

This was the backdrop to Lennon's childhood.

It was beautiful.

The burn of grief pulsed in Gabriele's chest. Why didn't he want to show her this?

The nippy wind whipped strands of hair across her face. She blew out sharply in response and jerked her head.

A tall, brick privacy wall covered in dry vines shielded the cottage from the house next door. It was a larger home about two or three times the size, but all she could see from her current vantage with clarity was a row of windows on the upper floor.

A sudden strong wind picked up the debris on the patio, blowing sand into Gabriele's face. She rushed inside, but the wind caught the door before she could grab the handle. She jumped when the door slammed shut with a loud bang. Her pulse beat in her ears until she calmed and was suddenly cloaked with quiet.

She leaned against the door. *This was his home.*

To the right was a cozy living room with plush furniture and a wood-burning stove in the corner. Gabriele had noted a small pile of chopped wood stacked along the house outside. The kitchen was open with a round wooden table and four chairs in the dining area. She returned to the end of the hallway to retrieve her bags and then opened the doors that led to a bathroom and two bedrooms.

Which one was his?

Odd. None of them had anything remotely personal in them to identify the room's primary occupant. Gabriele searched for photos or awards or yearbooks and found nothing, just neatly made beds and clutter-free cupboards.

Lennon must've had all personal items removed when he decided to sell it. The unease that lay like a nesting cobra in her belly rose. There were so many things she didn't understand about her husband. So many things she didn't *know*.

She chose the smaller one figuring the larger one would've belonged to the parents, and rolled in her suitcase. She sat quietly on the edge of the bed for several long moments.

Only that morning she'd awaken in her parents' flat in the *Neustadt*. It was late afternoon and now she was here on the coast of England. It was like another world, so different from Dresden. This was Lennon's world. This was Lennon's cottage.

Well, hers now. If she didn't sell it.

Which she probably would. Her family, her friends...they were in Dresden. Even though the cottage was cute and right on the beach, it wasn't her home. It hurt her heart to be here without Lennon.

It hurt to know that he hadn't wanted to show this to her

when he was alive.

Why?

Dust coated everything, so the first matter at hand was to give the place a good cleaning. She sighed with relief when she found a cupboard filled with cleaning supplies and an upright vacuum cleaner. She needed to keep busy. She needed to ignore the rising tide of emotions that threatened to take her out. She vacuumed and dusted, wiped down the cupboards, cleaned the bathroom, and washed the dishes in the cupboard. She cleaned until the cottage sparkled and she was a sweaty, grimy mess.

Gabriele ended with a shower, slipping into her pajama pants and a sweatshirt. She sat on the edge of the bed, wondering what she should do next. It was too early for bed and she hadn't thought about dinner. Her stomach was always rolling, hunger a thing she experienced only in the past, but she knew she should eat something. Her mama had packed her lunch. Maybe she'd eat that.

She reached over to the pillow, pinched the corner and pulled it to her face. It smelled clean, with a mild musky scent?

Lennon? Was this Lennon's scent? She sniffed it again. And again, filling her lungs. Was it him? She couldn't be sure. Was she forgetting him already? Oh, Lennon! Tears erupted, dampening the pillow, its official initiation into Gabriele's life.

Her phone rang, snapping her out of her weeping bout. A look at the call display confirmed it was her mama. She'd left her parents that morning at the Dresden Airport with looks of longing and worry following her as she passed through security and out of sight. They didn't understand why she felt she had to go, or why she had to go *so soon*. "You need to think this through, *Schatzi*."

HEART&SOUL

Her boss wasn't thrilled that Gabriele hadn't given proper notice before quitting, but they were heading into the off-season, and the museum had enough staff to cover her absence.

Gabriele lightened her voice and slipped into German. "Hello, Mama. No, I'm fine. I just got here... The flight was fine... The cottage is nice... I'm okay... The sea air will do me good... I don't know how long I'm staying... I should go... Take care."

The cottage had grown chilly and Gabriele remembered the wood stove. Dusk had fallen so she clicked on a floor lamp which cast a warm glow. She shrugged on her jacket and slipped into her shoes, heading out for the small woodpile she spotted by the door when she arrived. She filled her arms with as much as she could manage, choosing pieces of every size.

Gabriele dropped the pile of wood beside the stove. Now what? She'd never built a fire before. She had watched it done at bonfires, but that usually involved a bit of petrol.

She found a pack of matches in the corner along with a box of old newspapers. Her first effort was a colossal failure. The cottage filled with smoke and she had to sprint to open the terrace door to air it out.

The cottage filled with the cool, evening air and she shivered. This time she examined the stove more diligently. Ah, a closed vent. She opened it, rebuilt the teepee of kindling over the crumpled newspaper and struck the match.

Much better. She had to blow to encourage the spread of the flame, and then she carefully added wood, and soon she had a roaring fire. She left the front panel open, the protective screen in front, so she could watch the flames. It was like a spectacular screensaver, orange flames dancing, weaving in and out, but with a mesmerizing soundtrack of crackle and hiss noises.

If she focused hard she could clear her mind, forget the pain for a little while. She almost dozed off.

A face in the window.

Gabriele's head snapped up, her nerves on high alert.

Lennon?

For a split second she swore she saw his face. Rejecting the impossibility, Gabriele flew out the terrace door, eyes searching the darkness. "Lennon?"

A voluminous lump formed in her throat. She backed up slowly and closed the door. Sliding her back down its surface, she crouched and buried her face in her hands. Her mind had started playing tricks on her. She was going crazy.

Her tears turned to hard sobs and she wept bitterly into her sleeves. *Lennon, why did you have to go?*

THE HAPPY COUPLE

Then...

Gabriele Baumann-Smith.
Frau Smith.
Lennon and Gabriele Smith.
Mr. and Mrs. Smith.

She was a married woman! Gabriele grinned down at her super gorgeous husband as he lay bare-chested under a white sheet on a warm, late September evening. He threaded his fingers together and wrapped them behind his head exposing nicely-toned arms, and he unabashedly watched her through messy, almost-black hair that fell across dark eyes. Wearing pink boy-cut panties and a grey cotton tank-top, Gabriele hopped on the bed, her laptop in hand, and sat cross-legged beside him.

"The photographer finally sent us our pictures," she said with a happy lilt to her voice, and she flipped open the laptop. Its base warmed her bare legs as it whirled to life.

Lennon closed his eyes. "Don't be too disappointed. Pictures are never as good as the real thing."

"But this photographer came highly recommended." Gabriele clicked on the appropriate links and downloaded the files. "And I paid her good money." She held in a squeal. She was so excited to see these. Their wedding day had been perfect. Well, if she conveniently forgot about the tiny black mark put there by her drama-causing sister Eva and her famous boyfriend.

The laptop screen filled with thumbprint-sized icons and Gabriele clicked on the slideshow. She snuggled in close to Lennon. "Here we go!"

The first few shots were of the gathering crowds in the park on *An der Dreikönigsstrasse*. Some of the photos captured the blackened clock tower of Three Kings Church that poked the sunny, late August blue sky. Gabriele recognized almost everyone. She zoomed in on the faces of her childhood friends, family friends and distant relatives.

"There's Onkel Alfons and Tante Ruth. They came all the way from Freiberg. It was so good to see them again." A wave of sadness filled her when she recalled that Lennon wouldn't be able to pick out a familiar face. The whole ceremony had been for her sake since Lennon hadn't any family, something Gabriele found hard to imagine. He was an only child of only children. She almost burst into tears when he told her both of his parents had died. No wonder he didn't want to go back to England.

HEART & SOUL

Lennon would've been happy to have a simple civil ceremony with just the Baumann family present. "The honeymoon is the part I'm looking forward to," he'd said with a mischievous grin, but he gave in, somewhat begrudgingly, so she could have her own fairytale wedding.

The next several shots were of her in the upper room. Pre-service close-ups—her hair had been expertly styled with a fat-rod curling iron and decorated with diamond-like Zirconia pins that reflected the lighting. Her chiffon gown draped beautifully along her body landing delicately on the grey tiled floor.

The next collection of photos was of her friends fussing over her. Julia looked like a movie star with her short, dark hair pinned and curled, and with so much makeup on that Gabriele barely recognized her. There were a couple photos of Eva standing demurely nearby. She wore a lovely sage-green satin dress with daring, spaghetti-strap sleeves. Daring for her anyway. Her long, straight, milk chocolate brown hair was curled and pulled into an updo. She looked beautiful, yet pensive as she leaned on the white cane Gabriele had purchased for her for the occasion.

There were several more of Gabriele as she approached Lennon at the back of the church. The focus was on her. The shots were taken from Lennon's perspective, and he wasn't in the frames.

He squeezed her. "What a gorgeous bride!"

Gabriele smiled. "But where are you? I can't even tell you were there."

Lennon nibbled on her arm. "I only remember what

came after."

She laughed, but her eyes never left the screen. Finally, she came to a photo with Lennon in it. It was a profile shot of them standing together gazing lovingly at each other. Lennon looked spectacular in his shiny grey suit.

"So handsome," she said, "but your hair is hanging in your face." She had asked him more than once to get a haircut, but he insisted that he liked the longer look.

Shot after shot of the happy couple. A view from behind as they sat in the two chairs in the front of the sanctuary facing her papa as he conducted the ceremony. Many of them kissing.

"Oh, I like those ones," Lennon teased.

Gabriele felt a growing unease. So far she hadn't seen one good shot of both of them. None of Lennon at all.

The slideshow continued. In every single picture Lennon was looking down or behind or had hair in his eyes.

Gabriele huffed. "I don't believe this." She slumped against the pillow and bit her bottom lip. Disappointment was a black balloon in her chest. "Not even one picture of us worthy to hang on the wall!"

Lennon gently lifted the laptop and placed it on the floor beside him. "It's okay, Gabi. We can get more taken later."

Gabriele whimpered and tugged on her short bleach-blond hair. "It's not the same. I just don't understand how this happened. I know she took hundreds of pictures." She stared at Lennon. "How is it possible she missed getting one solid shot of your face?"

A dark look flashed behind Lennon's eyes. It only lasted

a split second, but Gabriele hadn't mistaken it. She'd seen it before. Not often, only a few times. It happened so seldom, she'd always pushed her concern away. It didn't mean anything.

It didn't.

Lennon reached over and turned out the light. "Get under the covers, love," he said. "Everything will look better in the morning."

FOAM FOR MY COFFEE

Gabriele awoke to natural light. She groaned, gripped the pillow from under her head, and planted it on her face to block the brightness. She breathed in the scent of the pillow and her eyes opened to the muffled darkness.

She inched the pillow off her face, remembering.

Lennon's cottage.

Her cottage.

A rumbling from her stomach. She hadn't eaten since breakfast the day before, and the lunch her mama had made her lay unopened on the dresser. The meat would be bad and the bread dry. She already knew there wasn't anything to eat in the cupboards.

What she really wanted was a coffee, unsweetened and topped with foamy milk. She remembered the coffee shop she passed the day before. They probably had a nice selection of pastries. That would work for a start, then later, when she had a chance to shower and dress, she'd go back in for groceries. It was only a ten-minute walk, and the exercise wouldn't hurt.

She gazed out the window, relieved to see the trees had stilled from a windless morning. The sun peeked over the horizon to the east, its rays dancing like diamonds over the much fuller sea. The tide was in and all the boats that had drooped over on the sand the evening before were upright and astute in the morning. She spotted a couple men in waders and with fishing equipment climbing into a small motorboat.

It promised to be a beautiful day.

Gabriele was tempted to just throw her jacket on over her pajamas but decided it wouldn't kill her to put on a pair of jeans.

The house still had a faint smoke smell from the fire she'd started the night before. It reminded her of her meltdown—had she actually believed she'd seen Lennon in the window? She shuddered.

Gabriele opened the terrace door and stopped. On the tiled deck directly in front of her was a tray, like a room service tray. There were two croissants and a biscuit, two tiny bowls, one with whipped butter and one with red jelly, a larger bowl with sliced fruit, and a carafe of coffee.

She cupped her eyes from the brightness of the sun and scanned her surroundings. She couldn't see anyone, but she noticed that someone had swept the leaves and sand off the terrace, and had draped a pretty floral tablecloth over the patio table.

What was going on?

A slip of paper had been tucked under the fruit bowl. She bent to remove it and read:

Welcome to the neighbourhood. I hope you enjoy your short time here.

If you need anything, let me know.

Your neighbour,
(house next door)
Callum Jones

Beneath the signature was a phone number.

Gabriele frowned. Here one day and already she had a stalker? And how did he know if her time here would be long or short?

She did appreciate the gesture, though. She picked up the tray and set it on the patio table. She noticed that the chairs had been wiped down, too. Whoever this Callum Jones guy was, he knew how to clean up.

She reached for the empty mug provided and let out a sigh. The neighbour wasn't so thorough after all, since he failed to provide milk or cream for her coffee. She wasn't sure if she could stomach it black, though she'd heard the British made it pretty weak. She poured the liquid in her cup and stared. It wasn't black, but a nice creamy color, and the milk had been *foamed*.

Her eyes darted to the house next door, to the windows that overlooked the cottage. She swore she saw someone in the closest one, standing behind the net curtains.

Was Callum Jones *watching* her?

A field of red flags sprang up. She almost took the tray and went inside, but then huffed. She was enjoying the morning sun seaside, an opportunity that didn't come to her often. She wasn't going to let a creepy neighbour rob her of that.

Though it did unnerve her that he knew how she took her coffee. How could he know that? She sniffed it. It smelled fine. Great, actually. Perhaps this was what small town hospitality looked like. She needed coffee and was willing to die for it. Figuratively speaking. She sighed and took a sip, deciding in that moment it didn't matter. The flavor was perfect.

Gabriele pulled out her phone so that the neighbour would see that she was just a keyboard away from dialing 999 if necessary. She texted Julia.

Gabriele Baumann-Smith
Sorry I didn't text last night. It was pretty emotional, but I'm okay. Drinking coffee on my patio. Watching sailboats bobbing in the distance.

Gabriele didn't expect an immediate response. Julia had a degree in Early Childhood Education and worked days as a kindergarten teacher.

The channel's cry was mellower today. The briny air invigorated her, and she actually felt a moment's peace as she let the sun's rays massage her face. Despite its dubious origins, the breakfast was lovely, and Gabriele was glad she hadn't had to make the trip into town: otherwise, she would've missed the melodic rhythm of the waves slapping the shore, the call of hungry sea birds, the warm saline air. Here she didn't have to deal with the mind-numbing chatter of strangers surrounding her, or waiting in a long queue. Or worry if she had enough British change. She almost forgot they didn't deal in Euros here, but remembered in time to have some converted at the airport before hiring the taxi.

But now what to do? Did Callum Jones really expect her to

call? What about his dishes? Gabriele didn't want him to come to collect them. Besides the fact that he'd already gone over and above the call of neighbourly duty, she would feel awkward. She didn't want to be put in a position where she had to make polite conversation. And she didn't know what, if anything, he'd want in return.

And it kind of creeped her out that he had entered her private property, her terrace, sometime in the early morning while she was sleeping.

TIME AND TROUBLE

He watched her through the upper-floor window, standing back from the net curtains to avoid being spotted prematurely. Her surprise at finding the breakfast he'd so painstakingly provided for her amused him.

He raised the mini binoculars to his eyes and examined the new neighbour. She was on the taller side for a woman, nice curves, heart-shaped face framed by silky auburn hair. Sure she was attractive, but so were millions of other women. What was so bewitching about this particular one?

She took the bait and sat outdoors. It was worth taking the time and trouble to clean it up. He wanted her outside so he could watch her.

Her expression when she poured her coffee moved quickly from surprised to suspicious. Her gaze cut to his window, and he made sure she glimpsed him before he drew back.

He wanted to startle her. Unsettle her. Make her uneasy.

His phone buzzed and he frowned at the text message. He had less time than he thought. He'd have to amp things up. Do whatever he had to do to run this woman out of town.

FAMILY DINNER

Then...

Gabriele and Lennon, *the Smiths* as Gabriele liked to think of their coupling now, had been attending Baumann family dinner on Monday evenings long before they were married. Today Mama had made roasted pork loin with gravy, potato dumplings, boiled red cabbage, and a rugola leaf salad with chopped orange and red peppers, sheep cheese, topped with a vinaigrette dressing. A basket of buns sat in the middle of the table.

Gabriele turned to Eva as she helped herself to the potato dumplings. "Where's Sebastian?"

Her sister handed her the bowl when she finished with it. "He's coming," she replied. "Hollow Fellows is recording at the Castle Studios in Röhrsdorf this week. He didn't know how long they'd be working today."

Hollow Fellows was the name of Sebastian Weiss's band. Gabriele had been very worried about her sister when he first showed up in her life, but now, the way Eva's green eyes sparkled with life every time she spoke of him, Gabriele knew she had no reason for concern. The look in Eva's eyes when she regarded Sebastian mirrored the look in Gabriele's similar green eyes when she thought of Lennon.

Lennon sat dutifully beside her, his usual quiet self. Her papa used to try to draw him out in conversation, resorting to comments about sports and politics, but after a while, he'd given up on small talk with his son-in-law.

Mama passed the buns around. Her short brunette bob was sprinkled with grey and deep lines fanned from the corners of her eyes when she smiled, which thankfully, was often. Papa sat at the head of the table, his broad shoulders rumbling as he laughed at something Eva said. Gabriele missed the joke. She'd been distracted by Lennon who was staring blankly ahead, his mind elsewhere.

She tapped his leg. "Is something wrong?"

"Oh, sorry, no." He smiled, but somehow it seemed forced. "Just daydreaming."

Eva caught Gabriele's eye. "When do you start your new job?"

"Tomorrow." Having recently finished her English and International Studies degree, Gabriele was happy to have finally landed a job, even if it was just as a tour guide at a local museum. She would be doing the English and French language tours and even though she hoped to do something more exciting with her linguistic skills, the museum was highly respected and would look good on her resume.

"Are you excited?"

"Yeah. It's a place to start."

The buzzer rang, indicating that someone was at the door of the building, two doors down. The Baumanns lived in a flat in a building facing the bustling *Alaunstrasse*, a floor above the street church where her parents ran a soup kitchen for the poor and working poor.

Eva jumped. "That's Sebastian."

Papa rose to push the button to let him in. His bushy eyebrows furrowed slightly like he wasn't yet used to his daughters being grown up with husbands and boyfriends.

Eva shifted her chair away from the table, gripped her cane that hung on the back and walked carefully to the door, reaching it just as Sebastian knocked.

She stepped into the hall to say her hellos privately.

"Get in here, you two," Papa growled playfully.

Eva giggled and they entered the room hand in hand.

"Hello, Baumann family and Smith family," Sebastian said with a contagious grin. "I hope I'm not too late."

"Of course not," Mama said, pointing to the empty chair with dishes in place. "We were expecting you."

The new-love affection Eva had for her boyfriend was so cute, Gabriele just had to get a picture. She removed her phone from her bag and pointed it. "Hey, you two!"

Eva squeezed in under Sebastian's arm and they both posed with wide grins.

Gabriele stared at the screen on her phone. "One, two, three."

"Now one of you guys," Eva offered. Gabriele handed her the phone. She pressed into Lennon who gave her an uncomfortable look. "Don't be shy," she teased. "He's got this weird camera phobia," she explained.

"I take awful pictures," Lennon said.

Gabriele poked him in the ribs. "Try smiling."

Eva counted, "*Eins, zwei, drei,*" then snapped.

Lennon lowered his head on three and Gabriele tensed. Her chest heated with a flicker of anger. He was a good-looking guy. Why couldn't he just cooperate?

"And one of Mama and Papa," she announced, standing. Lennon was sitting beside her mama and pulled away to remove himself from the shot. Gabriele didn't count it in. She clicked and checked the frame. She smiled. She purposefully didn't capture her parents.

Finally, she had a great face shot of Lennon.

UNNECESSARY BUT KIND

Gabriele washed the dishes and then decided on a shower. She intended to visit this Callum Jones person and thank him for his thoughtfulness. Meeting someone new meant putting a little effort into her looks.

Though, he might not be home. It was likely he had a job somewhere, right? That would be the best-case scenario. Gabriela picked up her pace. If she moved quickly she could avoid a face-to-face conversation.

Her hair was still a little damp when she left for the house next door, clean tray and dishes in hand. She could've gone to the streetside entrance, but since he'd trespassed on her terrace, she felt entitled to trespass on his. She carried the tray carefully down the wooden steps to the damp sand. A stone wall ran along the length of the beach protecting the occupants in the homes along the other side from high water flooding.

She stood on the sand, getting her first good look. Its larger size was obvious from this vantage point. The terrace was larger and sheltered, making it impossible to see if someone was on it or not. She'd spotted the two-car garage from the roadside the day before, but she was unable to tell if there was a vehicle inside to ascertain if someone were home. She hesitated a moment before climbing the stairs. The Jones's terrace was large and housed a patio set and a bar-b-que, both covered in tarps and tied down, giving Gabriele the impression that Mr. Jones didn't spend a lot of time at his beach house this time of year. A large security sign hung in the window. She tentatively knocked on the door, not wanting to inadvertently set off an alarm. From the corner of her eye she saw an upper-level curtain move in an open window.

She waited, and when the door remained unanswered, she knocked again, harder this time.

Nothing.

Gabriele stared up at the window. The curtain flicked from the morning breeze. She must've imagined movement. Mr. Jones wasn't home.

Feeling a mix of relief and disappointment, she placed the tray in front of the door.

Scheisse. She'd forgotten to write a note. She tugged her mobile from out of her jeans pocket and pulled up the number she'd entered for Callum Jones. She hadn't intended to use it to say thank you. It felt too... friendly. And she didn't want to be this guy's friend.

She sighed. Maybe she was reading too much into things. The guy was just being a nice neighbour. Not likely a rapist or a murderer.

She could just leave the dishes and say thankyou later, but

that could be construed as rude. Who knew when she'd see him again? If she had her way, it would be a long time from now. Like never. She could go back for a note... oh, she was being neurotic. Just get it over with and move on.

Gabriele Baumann-Smith
Thank you for the lovely breakfast. It was unnecessary but kind.

To the point, but not excessive.

It wasn't until she reached the door of her cottage that it occurred to her that she'd just given the man her name and her number.

THAT IS CRAZY THINKING

Then...

Gabriele buttoned up a freshly pressed white cotton blouse and slipped into black dress pants. Today was her first day at her new job as a tour guide at the Turkish Museum in the *Altstadt*. "One of the oldest and most important collections of Ottoman art anywhere in the world outside Turkey," she'd explained to Lennon. She had spent the last three days studying the information, not wanting to get even one little fact wrong, and practicing the whole tour in English the night before with Lennon.

In fact, their relationship language was primarily English. When they first met just over a year ago, Lennon didn't speak any German at all. Fortunately, Gabriele studied English all through school and majored in languages at university, so starting a friendship with Lennon wasn't difficult, as long as it was in English.

Lennon put forth a good effort in learning German. For whatever reason, he wanted to stay in Germany, though Gabriele had suggested they move to England for a little while, just for the experience.

Lennon had gently but firmly said no, and she understood why. Too many painful memories.

"What do you think?" Gabriele swiveled to present herself to Lennon who was also preparing to leave for his job with a small IT firm.

"You look smashing." He tied a black tie while eying her. "Very tour guide-ish."

She stepped close to help him center his tie and brushed her lips against his. "You look super smashing."

He grabbed her by the hip bones and pressed her against his body. "And you look super, super smashing." He pronounced "super" the German way, *zoopah*, and Gabriele laughed.

"Okay, back off big guy," she said, pushing his chest gently. "I've got to get ready."

Gabriele prepared her first cup of coffee of the day, which she planned on drinking while she did her hair and makeup. Lennon drank tea, so she plugged in the kettle for him.

She stepped into their small living room while she waited. "Should I make reservations?"

He glanced up from the BBC news program he watched

every morning. "For what?"

"Our one-month anniversary. Since we were married." They'd gone out the night before with other people, but Gabriele wanted a nice one-on-one celebration, too.

"Oh. Oh? Yeah, sure. Make reservations. Where are we going?"

Gabriele named the restaurant they went to when she and Lennon had first decided to get married.

"Nice choice. Good memories there."

The whistle blew, and Gabriele lifted the kettle from its base and poured Lennon his tea. He never asked her to do this, but she didn't mind. It only took her a minute more while she made her coffee anyway.

"Here you go," she said as she handed him the hot mug.

He smiled, taking the cup. "Thanks, love." His attention then immediately returned to the news program. Gabriele caught the headline: *terrorism in England on the rise: recent threat of domestic terrorism thwarted.*

Gabriele sipped her coffee and took a moment to drink in the sight of her handsome husband. He leaned forward on their new Ikea sofa with elbows on denim-clad thighs. He'd rolled up the sleeves of his white dress shirt and his black tie hung down, precariously close to being dipped into his cup of tea. His hair was long and shaggy on top but short around his ears and the back of his neck. She still couldn't believe she'd landed such a gorgeous guy. That they, in fact, were *married.*

She played with the gold band on her finger. She doubted the novelty would ever rub off. She loved being a wife. She loved being *his* wife.

The living room housed most of their belongings: the new sofa with two contrasting chairs, an area rug with a square coffee table in the middle. A couple modern art prints hung on white walls. Gabriele's guitar rested on a stand in the corner. She loved shopping together with Lennon as they planned decorating and outfitting their first home. It was Gabriele's first time living away from her parents, straight from a papa to a husband, but she didn't mind missing out on living on her own. She was one of the lucky ones. She found her soul mate early in life.

Her eyes landed on the empty frame that leaned against the wall on the floor and her smile fell. They must be the only couple on the planet who didn't have one decent wedding photo to hang. She shoved down the pang and returned to the kitchen to prepare toast.

"Gabi!" Lennon's voice had that irritated edge he'd acquired recently.

"Yeah?" she called back.

Lennon stormed into the kitchen. "You took a picture of me yesterday? Why did you post it on Facebook? You know how I feel about that."

Gabriele scowled and threw her shoulders back. "What's the big deal? I can't post any pictures? Am I supposed to just drop off social networking altogether?"

Gabriele let out a huff of hurt and frustration. Lennon was a private person, she knew that. Some people really didn't like getting their pictures taken. She had a number of friends who claimed to not be photogenic and hated every photo taken of them. They were just overcritical of their looks, picking out every imperfection.

Gabriele wasn't like that. She liked having her picture taken. She liked sharing pieces of her life with her friends online. And Lennon was a big part of her life.

"I'm not trying to be difficult," Lennon said quietly.

"Then why are you? They're just pictures."

"I don't like it."

Gabriele sighed. "But you're my husband. And you're hot. I just want to show you off."

Lennon's head fell forward and his shoulders slumped. He tugged on Gabriele's sleeve and pulled her into an embrace.

"I'm sorry. I just wish you wouldn't."

Gabriele forced herself to hug Lennon back. She didn't understand why they were fighting over something so silly. She and Lennon had been practically inseparable over the last year, and she was certain she knew him well. But, maybe she didn't. Maybe he had a weird kind of phobia or OCD or childhood trauma that was triggered by picture-taking.

She'd thought it odd and unfortunate that she and Lennon happened to book a hotel in Greece that didn't have internet. Lennon consoled her when she complained, saying he didn't want the rest of the world with them on their honeymoon anyway. Then she lost her phone on the last day and all the pictures she'd taken with it.

Lennon had tried to comfort her back then. But what if he had meant for it to happen all along? He *was* the last one to use her phone.

Stop! That is crazy thinking.

Shame blanketed her. How could she doubt her husband in this way? It was all just an unfortunate coincidence.

Stupid pictures weren't worth ruining what they had in real life.

"It's fine," she said, breaking away. "I'll try to be more sensitive."

Gabriele quickly ate breakfast and brushed her teeth. Lennon's job started early so he was the first to leave.

"Have a great first day," he said. He ducked down as she wrapped her arms around his neck to kiss him goodbye. He felt tense, and not for the first time Gabriele wondered if she'd done something wrong.

"Are you okay?" she asked.

He leaned back and peered into her eyes. His expression softened. "Of course. Things are just hectic at work, that's all. We'll have a nice dinner tonight."

Gabriele relaxed in his arms. Everything was okay. She was just being oversensitive.

Lennon kissed her again, long and slow. He whispered in her ear. "Maybe we should call in sick."

On another day, Gabriele would've acquiesced. She didn't like this "thing" that had developed between them, and a day off to make love would be just what they needed.

She smiled. "I wish we could, but I can't skip out on my first day. Now off you go."

Then...

Gabriele was exhausted by the time her shift ended at the museum. She enjoyed interacting with the customers, but after her third recitation of the facts, she was already bored. Was this what she'd spent five years in uni to do? Surely, there was something else out there for her. Something more exciting and challenging.

Her feet and her back hurt from walking and standing and her voice was hoarse from talking so much. She almost regretted making dinner plans, but at least she had a couple hours to rest at her flat before Lennon got home from work.

But first she'd stop to say a quick hello to her mama. Mama had made her promise to come by on her way home to tell her all about her first day at work.

HEART & SOUL

Gabriele biked down *Alaunstrasse* where you had a greater chance of being hit by a cyclist than you did by a car, and she dodged a pedestrian who failed to look both ways as she crossed from the flower shop to the small, sparse park where the headbangers liked to hang out with their large dogs.

Gabriele parked her bicycle in the rack in the courtyard at the back of the building and climbed the cement stairwell to the second-floor flat she'd lived in with her parents and sister for eight years.

It felt strange to knock on the door, but she tapped it lightly before letting herself in.

"Mama?"

"Gabriele! Come in."

"Hi, Mama."

"So nice to see you. I'm baking cookies."

"Smells great." She slumped gratefully into a kitchen chair. "Where's Papa?"

It was her parents' day off from working in the soup kitchen/house church, which explained the baking.

"He's visiting a fellow in need of counseling and support," her mama answered

So not a day off for him. Gabriele smiled. Her papa loved helping people.

Mama pushed a plate of homemade sugar cookies across the table towards her. "How was your first day?"

Gabriele reached for a cookie. "Okay. My nerves settled down after I completed the first circuit. The people I work with are nice. My new boss is nice." She stretched out her legs. "But my back and my feet are killing me."

"Rest a little, *Schatzi*. Do you want something to drink?"

Gabriele smiled. She'd become a guest since leaving home and getting married. Normally, it would be expected that she would serve herself.

"*Sprudelwasser, bitte*," she replied, and her mother brought her a glass of bubbly, mineral water.

Mama sat in the chair beside her, watching. "So, how is everything?"

What did she mean by "How is *everything?*" Could her mama tell that something was off between Lennon and her? Gabriele adjusted her expression. "Everything is good. Lennon's good. We're good."

Mama nodded and smiled gently. "It's normal for the first few months after marriage to be… tricky. So many new adjustments."

"We're adjusting," Gabriele said stiffly. Then she added with a forced smile, "We're going for dinner tonight to celebrate our first month being married."

Mama patted her hand. "That's wonderful."

It was wonderful. She was blowing everything out of proportion. Lennon was kind and gentle, supportive and encouraging. So he didn't like getting his picture taken. So what. Such a small thing in light of everything else he offered her.

They were adjusting. That was all. Adjusting.

Gabriele's smile returned, genuine this time. "I should go home and get ready." She kissed her Mama on the cheek. "Until later."

HEART&SOUL

Gabriele showered, brushed her teeth and crawled under the covers in nothing but her underwear. She had an hour before Lennon got home and she just needed a short nap to recover from first-day-at-work jitters.

They lived on the top floor of an old house that had been converted into three flats. Gabriele stared at the skylight in the slanted, open-vaulted ceiling, and tried to imagine what she was going to feel like after doing the museum tour over and over again, week after week, month after month.

Gabriele groaned. She could do this job for awhile, but she'd have to keep looking for something else. She didn't worry about it for too long before dozing off.

She overslept. Somewhere in her subconscious, she could feel him watching her. Her eyes flickered open to find Lennon standing at the foot of the bed, staring. The sheets had shifted during her sleep, baring a leg and most of her torso.

"God, you're beautiful." His expression was feral, his eyes dark. Without removing his gaze from her, he undid his tie and tossed it to the floor. Then he slowly unbuttoned his shirt.

Wearing just his jeans low on his hips, he crawled on top of her, bearing his weight on his arms. His eyes were intense, glassy with emotion. His gaze spiked her, held her still. Only her heart remained in motion, beating out of control. His lips lowered to hers and he kissed her deeply. His mouth moved hungrily along her chin and down her neck, and her back arched in attention. His hands moved delicately along her body like he was imprinting her to memory, igniting every nerve.

The intensity of his hunger and need overwhelmed her. She'd never seen this side of him. Never knew this existed. She was too breathless to speak. She let go of all her inhibitions, matching his passion in her expression, giving herself, losing herself. Loving him.

They missed their reservation.

Lennon flopped on his back, breathing deeply. Gabriele pulled the sheets up under her chin, feeling stunned by Lennon's aggressive lovemaking. He'd never devoured her like this before. It excited and frightened her.

He rolled onto his side and stroked her hair. "Are you okay?"

She turned onto her side to face him. "Yeah, are you?"

"Never better." He kissed her head. "But now I'm starving."

Food was the last thing on her mind, but now that Lennon had mentioned it, her stomach woke up and growled. "Me, too."

"I'll run out for gyros," he said. He jumped out of bed and dressed. Gabriele just nodded and mumbled. She hadn't fully recovered from Lennon's ravenous love making. Anything he said would be fine by her.

She roused herself out of bed and dressed in her

pajamas. It was early in the evening, but she didn't feel like putting on clothes. She brushed her teeth and washed her face, applying a touch of mascara. Lennon obviously didn't mind her bare face, but she felt better with a little makeup on. After what they just experienced together, she wanted to look good for him when he returned.

She checked her phone and found a text from Julia asking if Gabriele wanted to go shopping with her sometime and one from Eva thanking her for the picture she'd sent of her and Sebastian from the night before.

She checked the time. Lennon had been gone forty-five minutes. The gyros restaurant was just down the street. He was normally there and back within twenty minutes.

Another twenty minutes passed and she picked up her phone once again, intending to text him, but before she had a chance, a text came in from him.

Lennon Smith
No matter what happens, I love you.

Gabriele froze. No matter what happens? What did Lennon mean by that?

Gabriele Baumann-Smith
What do you mean? What's happening?

She waited for a response but when none came, she texted again.

Gabriele Baumann-Smith
Where are you??

She couldn't fight the dense wave of rising panic. Something was wrong. Why didn't he text her back?

Gabriele Baumann-Smith
Lennon?!

WRONGLY BELIEVED

Gabriele spent the morning walking up and down the beach. It was too cold to go barefoot, and even with the sun shining, she needed to keep her jacket zipped. She was fascinated with the ocean life the sea discarded on the shore: seaweed, shells, driftwood.

Gabriele imagined Lennon playing here as a boy. Fishing in a little dingy. Sailing. Maybe he brought his girlfriends to the pond on the other side of Callum Jones's house. Close, but out of sight.

Her heart squeezed. Lennon never spoke of a specific girlfriend. Now that Gabriele thought about it, everything Lennon ever told her about his past was in broad, vague strokes. He told her he lived in England, outside of London, but not specifically where. Same with schools, no full names of friends. He worked at a car wash growing up, but Gabriele couldn't say which one. She didn't see a car wash here in Emsworth.

They had talked a lot about music, books and current events. Her schooling and their wedding. Always about the moment, but hardly anything about the past. And very little about the future, Gabriele realized. Except that Lennon made it clear he wanted to settle down into a quiet life, something Gabriele had agreed to consider *after* they had a little adventure.

She had been extremely busy with university and then with wedding plans. The truth was, she and Lennon were only together for a year before they wed. She loved him, that was undeniable, but had she really *known* him?

She had wrongly believed that she'd have the rest of her life to get to know him. Now she never would.

She wiped at tears that dampened her face and she headed back to the cottage. She needed to buy a few groceries as it was unlikely that another neighbour would be so kind as to bring her lunch. She headed out the backdoor to the narrow road and into town.

Gabriele paused at the corner that intersected with a main road and stared once again at the pub. It had white plaster walls with dark wood framing an old door with wrought-iron hinges. Across the street was a key-cutting shop tucked between a Chinese takeaway restaurant on one side and a natural herbs store on the other. The sandwich sign on the pavement in front of her informed Gabriele that open mic night was tomorrow. Not for the first time, she wished she'd brought her guitar. Impulsively, she stepped inside.

The room had low ceilings and was dimly lit. The interior walls, like the exterior, were whitewashed with exposed dark beams running along. High shelves housed a collection of beer mugs and other mementos.

Most of the tables were full with patrons eating lunch. Gabriele smelled the strong vinegary scent of fish and chips. According to the chalk-drawn menu hanging on the wall behind the bar, seafood was a specialty.

A redheaded girl about Gabriele's age manned the bar. Her eyes were very dark, almost black and she wore no makeup which made them appear even more prominent against her silky white skin and high cheekbones. Her name tag read Ciara. She flashed Gabriele a smile revealing a row of very nice, white teeth.

"Can I get you something?" The girl's voice had a playful, Irish lilt to it. Gabriele couldn't help but smile back.

"Uh, no. I'm, I was just passing by."

"Sure. Take a look around. Let me know if you change your mind."

"Thanks," Gabriele said as she moved towards the door. The atmosphere appealed to her. Maybe she would come tomorrow night to listen to the local talent.

Gabriele put on her sunglasses the minute she stepped outside. She noticed a man standing on the corner, broad shouldered in a navy blue jacket, a black cap on his head, and dark sunglasses on his face. He spun away, turning his back to her the moment she glanced at him and then he disappeared.

Not everyone in Emsworth was the friendly sort.

She took her time in the grocery store, amusing herself with all the different kinds of foods. She was disappointed by the lack of "real" bread, the dark, dense, seedy kind she loved to eat back home, but allowed herself to be adventurous and try something new. At least the fruits and vegetables were recognizable.

She almost bought too much to carry and made a note to buy less next time and make extra trips if necessary.

She blinked twice, sure she'd seen the man in the blue coat again. He'd disappeared behind a service van, and when the vehicle passed, the man was gone.

Gabriele broke out in goose pimples. Was someone following her?

SOMETHING'S WRONG

Then...

Gabriele put a hand to the hard pounding in her chest. She stood frozen to the spot, unsure of what to do next. Call the police? And tell them her husband just texted her a strange love note? That he's been gone for less than two hours?

Instinctively she knew she should get dressed. Whatever explanation Lennon had for her when he got home, she didn't want to be wearing her pajamas when she heard it.

Gabriele dug through her wardrobe until she found a clean pair of jeans and then slipped a comfortable, light knit cardigan over her head.

She brushed her hair and worked a palm full of mousse into the strands, giving it life. She examined her dark roots.

She'd have to get another cut and colour soon.

The mirror only distracted her for so long. Her stomach stirred with sour juices. Where was Lennon?

She checked her phone again. No new messages.

No matter what happens, I love you.

Gabriele's heart thudded in her chest. Lennon hadn't been himself lately. Now that she thought about it, he'd seemed quieter than usual. Tense. Was he in some kind of trouble? Why hadn't he confided in her? Wasn't that what married couples did?

She lowered herself onto the sofa and waited. She repeatedly checked the time on her phone. She called and left another message on his voice mail.

A thick knot of dread brewed in her belly. *Lennon.*

Down deep she knew. She just *knew.*

A knock on the door. Oh, God. Lennon wouldn't knock.

Her legs were like lead, barely able to carry her through the growing emotional smog. She opened the door, and her eyes burned at the sight of the two policemen standing there.

"Are you Frau Gabriele Baumann-Smith?"

Gabriele nodded once.

"There has been a shooting incident. We regret to inform you that your husband, Lennon Smith, has been killed."

I THINK IT'S TIME

The bulky weight of the grocery bags in her arms caused Gabriele to navigate the walk back slowly. Her heart jumped when she arrived at the front door. A guitar case sat on the step. Gabriele dumped her bag of groceries on the ground beside it. A white piece of paper trapped under the instrument flickered in the breeze. She snapped it out and read:

I heard you like to play guitar.

Please feel free to borrow mine for the length of your stay.

Callum

Gabriele's heart jumped with anxiety. Who *was* this guy? She felt more than a little unnerved by the fact that this man, this *stranger,* seemed to know so much about her. If he was trying to freak her out, it was working.

Gabriele stepped around the guitar to bring the groceries inside and put them away. Then she went outside, and stared at the guitar case.

It looked expensive. Unmarred. Almost new. It wasn't new, was it? He didn't buy it just for her to play, did he?

Oh, God.

Was he the guy in the blue jacket?

Gabriele twisted to scan the trees and the walled area that divided the cottage from the house. She stared up at the upper-floor windows. Was he watching her from there?

A rush of cool adrenaline flooded her chest. She no longer felt safe sitting outside alone.

She almost left the guitar outside on the step, but feared Callum Jones would come over if he spotted it left outside. She carried it in and locked the door.

Tears burned at the back of her eyes. Maybe she should go back to Germany sooner than later. Sell the cottage like Lennon had wanted her to. He must've had a reason not to tell her about this place, and Gabriele wouldn't doubt if those reasons had something to do with the elusive, yet intrusive, overly generous neighbour.

Her fear was slowly eclipsed by indignation. Who did this guy Callum Jones think he was? Why would she let him, someone she hadn't even met, scare her away? She would go back to Germany when she was good and ready. She would sell or not sell because she decided to, not because she felt pushed out.

Gabriele's nerves settled enough that she could make herself a pot of soup and even managed to force down a soft sweet bun. She made coffee, foaming the milk with the hand foamer she'd brought with her and then stared at the guitar case where she'd left it in the living room.

She wouldn't play it. Tomorrow morning, hoping Callum Jones had a job and would be at work, she'd drop it off with a "thanks, but no thanks" note.

By mid-afternoon, Gabriele was already exhausted. The events of the last few days had taken their toll. Her adrenaline rush had lapsed and fatigue had rushed in to replace it. She meant to lie down for just a few minutes, but when she awoke, it was already dark.

She fumbled with the lamp on the nightstand, feeling momentarily discombobulated, before remembering once again where she was and why.

She went through the motions of starting a fire, no mishaps this time, and made herself a cheese and tomato sandwich.

Gabriele's eyes darted back to the guitar case. She sighed. Since the guitar was here anyway, she might as well try it out.

Out the window she could see the night sky was clear, sprinkled with a host of sparkling stars. She stared at them and thought of Lennon. He was in a better place. She had told herself this over and over again over the last year. She thought maybe now she was starting to believe it.

She unbuckled the case and gasped. Inside was a classic Fender. She picked it up gently and cradled it on her lap. The mahogany top was smooth and unmarred. The strings were new, and she spent a few minutes tuning, running her fingers along the rosewood fingerboard, then she began plucking, filling the cottage with its warm, bright tone.

She hummed a tune, letting new words tumble in her mind. She quickly reached for her notebook sitting on the coffee table and began to scribble.

We say that the stars are just
Holes in the night sky
Letting the light shine in
From a better world

She played and wrote furiously until her fingers ached and the fire in the woodstove died out. Once she felt the song was done, or at least as done as she was capable of doing in one sitting, she put the guitar back into its case and buckled the snaps, feeling the sense of euphoria that came with creating something.

Her phone buzzed on the table where she'd left it. Eva again, she assumed. Her family worried about her so much.

She froze when she saw the name.

Callum Jones
Gabriele, is the guitar to your liking?

Gabriele collapsed into a chair. Why hadn't she taken the time to write and deliver a stupid thank-you note for the breakfast? Texting her gratitude was a dumb thing to do.

Should she answer or ignore?

Ignore.

Ten minutes later.

Callum Jones
Perhaps I've overstepped. If you don't like it, just leave it on the step and I'll collect it in the morning before work.

So, he did work. Which meant he didn't spend his days following her. Now she felt stupid and ungrateful.

HEART&SOUL

Gabriele Baumann-Smith
It's very nice. Thanks.

Callum Jones
I hear you are the new owner of the cottage and want to sell. I may know of a buyer.

How did he know that?

Gabriele Baumann-Smith
How do you know that?

Callum Jones
It's a small town. People talk.

Oh. Was that all there was to it?

Gabriele Baumann-Smith
I'd be curious to know who knew I liked foamed milk in my coffee or that I played guitar. Especially, since I didn't arrive with a guitar and had yet to order a coffee in town.

Callum Jones
It's best if you just sell and be on your way.

Now Gabriele was annoyed. She wasn't about to be told what to do by a virtual stranger.

Gabriele Baumann-Smith
What makes you think I want to sell?

Callum Jones
You want to. Trust me.

Gabriele huffed.

Gabriele Baumann-Smith
Why should I trust you? And for the record, I don't.

Another ten minutes passed and Gabriele thought maybe she'd shaken him. Then her phone buzzed again.

Callum Jones
I think it's time we met.

Gabriele Baumann-Smith
I don't think so.

Callum Jones
I'm coming over now.

Gabriele Baumann-Smith
If you do, I'll call the police.

Callum Jones
You don't want to do that.

Gabriele Baumann-Smith
I think maybe I do.

The lock on the terrace door clicked and the door inched open. Gabriele screeched. A man stood in the doorway with a mobile clenched in one hand and a key in the other.

"I don't mean to scare you," he said, "but there's no good way to do this."

The blood drained to Gabriele's feet as she gawked at his familiar face. "L-lennon?"

"I'm not Lennon. I'm his twin brother."

BLIND, DEAF, DROWNING

Gabriele grabbed at her chest, a rattling tin can, and tried to catch her breath. She paced the floor with short jagged steps, casting piercing glances at the man before her, the man who looked exactly like her husband.

She felt faint and her forehead grew damp.

She sat. Then stood.

She stared hard at Callum Jones. He looked so much like Lennon. It took all her willpower not to throw herself into his arms. "Oh, my God," she said breathlessly. "Why didn't he tell me about you?"

"He had his reasons."

"His *reasons*? I am his wife! This is a pretty big secret!"

She sat again. Frowning, she took a long look at her husband's brother. On second thought they weren't *exactly* the same. Where Lennon had hair long enough to cover his face,

Callum's, though the same dark colour, was much shorter. Where Lennon was lean and walked with a relaxed swagger, Callum was bulkier like he spent a lot of time working out. He stood straight with his shoulders back, not at all relaxed.

Where Lennon smiled, at least when looking at Gabriele, Callum's expression remained stern. It was Lennon's face, but rock hard. When Lennon had watched her, his gaze was always filled with adoration. Callum's eyes were filled with something else. Distrust? Dislike?

"I need an explanation," she finally said.

"I'm afraid I can't give you one."

"I'm not leaving until I get some answers."

Callum folded his hands in front of his chest. "I'll collect you in the morning and deliver you to the airport myself. Good-day."

Like a storm, he left as abruptly as he came. Gabriele felt like she'd just been hit by a tidal wave, her feet knocked out from under her, her body twisting and jerking under silt-strewn water. Blind. Deaf. Drowning.

Nights Are Long

Then...

Quiet and solitude. That was all Gabriele wanted. Somehow she'd made it through the funeral. It was sad, much like her wedding had been, in that all the people who had come were there for her. Lennon didn't have anybody but her.

It was like she had married a ghost.

She curled up in a tight knot in the bed she'd shared with Lennon. It felt too big now. She could spread eagle her arms and legs—there was space enough, but the act made her feel exposed and vulnerable. She was like a newborn who found comfort in her strange, new scary world by curling up in a fetal position, knees to chin, thighs pressed against her chest, containing the pain.

It had been a week already, and she still couldn't believe

he was gone. When she closed her eyes, she could imagine him lying beside her. She often moved in and out of restless sleep where he'd meet her. She'd stretch out her arm to touch him, only to be reminded like a cold slap to the face that he wasn't there.

Every morning she'd wake up and listen for the sound of the shower, evidence that Lennon was still with her, that her life hadn't been randomly tossed upside down, that she wasn't in some kind of horrific, haunted fairground ride, spinning her around and around out of control.

Sometimes her dreams were so real, she could smell his skin and taste his mouth. She'd sit up breathless, only to remember the horrible truth that Lennon was gone.

He knew. She didn't know how but he *knew*. That last night when he loved her like he was dying, like he'd never see her again, he was saying *good-bye*.

A deep moan escaped from an unquenchable place in her soul.

If she could only just sleep and sleep and sleep and never wake up. They could be together again.

She curled up tighter.

Her phone buzzed on the mattress by her pillow. She knew who it was. It was always the same person.

Eva Baumann
Do you want company?

Gabriele Baumann-Smith
I just want to be alone.

Eva Baumann
Mama and I could come with a meal.

Gabriele groaned. The last thing she needed was to engage in small talk, meaningless banter about anything and everything that wasn't Lennon.

Gabriele Baumann-Smith
I just want to be alone.

Eva Baumann
You can't hole up alone forever.

Gabriele Baumann-Smith
I'm not asking for forever. I'm just asking for today.

And tomorrow. And maybe forever.

Eva Baumann
Okay. I'll check in tomorrow.

Gabriele Baumann-Smith
Okay.

>Maybe.

VALUABLE AND WASTED

Callum waited in the darkened second-story room, awake long before the first light in the cottage went on. Gabriele was up in plenty of time to make the first flight out of London to Dresden and Callum grinned smugly. This was going to be easier than he thought.

He'd gone for the jugular the night before, and a small part of him felt badly for the girl. Her anguish was clear. He had dropped a bomb and then left without helping the wounded.

He sipped his coffee and checked the time. He couldn't wait until it was time to pick her up. He just wanted to get this over with.

Callum didn't doubt that Gabriele was a nice girl. His brother had only been attracted to nice girls. But Mick was gone now, and his widow was partly to blame for that—a fact that coated his heart with lacquer, making him more eager than ever to ship her away for good.

HEART&SOUL

Unless he could use her to lure his brother's killers out in the open? Had Mrs. *Smith* stayed in Germany she would've remained under the radar. They'd silenced the one who could testify and had the power to send them all to prison. Mick was the only one they had cared about.

But if they found out his wife was here in England, they might make a move, purely out of revenge or whatever other insane reasonings they had for all the things they did. If he played his cards right, using Gabriele Baumann as bait, he could nail them once and for all.

Tempting.

Except that he'd promised his brother to keep her safe. And that meant returning her to Germany before their enemies knew she was on British soil.

The sale of the cottage could proceed. Callum didn't resent his brother too much for leaving it to his wife. Callum had enough money and though it would've been nice to continue to rent the cottage, he was also ready to be relieved of the responsibility.

He couldn't wait to get back to his flat in London, back to the work that awaited him there. His colleagues were more than capable, but he didn't like the feeling that he wasn't pulling up his share of the workload. The time he spent here chasing Gabriele away was valuable and wasted.

The terrace door of the cottage opened, and Callum sat up. Gabriele's pretty head stuck out and she looked up at his window. He pulled back slightly even though he knew she couldn't see him sitting in the dark, especially behind the net curtains.

Gabriele exited and locked the door. She glanced up at him

one more time and then skipped on the stairs to the beach and took off at a jog.

What the hell?

Callum sprinted down the stairs, grabbing his blue jacket on his way out. He shrugged it on while jogging, and removed the hat and glasses from his pockets and put them on. It wasn't so early that people weren't out and about, and he was recognizable. His family had lived in Emsworth for a long time, and his dad had been well known and respected in the community. If anyone recognized Callum, they wouldn't hesitate to pull him over to chat, especially in light of the tragic circumstances that surrounded him. Callum was one of theirs. He pulled his cap down lower.

He caught sight of her purple autumn jacket and slowed his pace. It wasn't like he could drag her by the hair to the airport. He pulled his stunt the night before hoping that she'd want to run back to her mama in Germany. She had more gumption that he'd given her credit for. He regretfully acknowledged a sprig of admiration.

He turned the corner by 36 on the Quay and panicked when he didn't spot her on the road. That girl was moving more quickly than he'd thought. He broke into a jog, hoping to catch sight of her around the curve in the road but couldn't spot her auburn ponytail anywhere.

IN LIGHT OF US

After a restless night of fitful sleep, Gabriele found herself sitting blurry eyed on a tall stool at the bar in the Irish Pub. She'd outsmarted her neighbour by taking the long route and circling back to the pub. Bike riding to work in Dresden had kept her in shape. She smirked. Callum Jones could take the next flight to Dresden and shove it.

Gabriele had started with coffee, two cups, then had switched to beer. It was only midmorning.

"It's pretty early to be drinking," the bartender said, sliding a pint across the counter. He was lean with pale skin and black hair. His face was attractive, with dark brows over grey eyes, a strong jaw and a flirty smile.

She took a sip and wiped foam off her lips with the back of her hand. "It's nighttime somewhere in the world."

"Indeed it is." He extended his hand. "The name's Riley."

She shook it in response. "Gabriele."

"Where ya from, Gabriele?"

"Germany. Let me guess. You're from Ireland."

"Ah, she's astute and beautiful."

Gabriele let out a guffaw. She usually considered herself attractive, but not today. She didn't even bother to put on her makeup and she knew her eyes were bloodshot and frightful.

She was just finishing her second beer when the redheaded girl, Ciara, began a new shift. She had her hair swept up in a messy copper bun, like she'd forgone her brush and used her fingers instead. Gabriele liked her.

"Oh, good," Riley began, "the help has arrived. Finally."

The girl smirked and took her spot behind the bar.

"This is our guest Gabriele," he continued. "I'll leave you in Ciara's capable hands."

"Hi, Ciara," Gabriele said with a slight slur, "I'd like another."

Ciara cocked a brow, then placed a clean mug under the spigot. "I'm only serving ya because I know you can walk home from here."

"How do you know that?" Gabriele demanded. "How does everyone already know my business? I've only been here for one and a half days!"

Ciara laughed and slid the frosty mug across the bar. "It's a small town."

Gabriele grunted. "So I've heard. With your name and your accent, I gather you aren't a local either."

"Nah. But my brother bought this place. I came for a summer job and have been here for two years now."

Gabriele narrowed her eyes as her gazed moved from Ciara to Riley. "That's your brother?"

"Uh-huh."

His hair colour was different than Ciara's but Gabriele could see the resemblance.

"I take it you're from Germany?" Ciara asked.

"Is my accent that strong?"

"Not really. Small town, remember?"

"Dresden." Gabriele lowered her voice and cricked her finger, calling Ciara closer. She whispered conspiratorially. "How much do you know about the Jones brothers?"

Ciara shook her head and whispered back. "Don't know no Jones brothers."

"What about Smith brothers?"

Ciara shrugged. "Jones and Smith are very popular surnames. Nothing jumps out to me." She tilted her head and arched an auburn brow. "Do these brothers have something to do with your choice of breakfast?"

Gabriele grunted. "You could say that."

"I can get you eggs and toast."

That sounded good, but before Gabriele could respond her attention was grabbed by a stir behind her. The pub had been filling up with patrons looking for breakfast. A cute blond girl had entered and pulled up a seat at a crowded table. The guys and girls there seemed quite taken with her.

"Who's that?" Gabriele asked.

"Now there's a story," Ciara said. "That's Clover Swift. She dated a guy straight through year ten and into uni. One day, he just disappeared. Poof. And only a week after his father had passed. People still talk about it. Some think he went off the deep end, just unable to handle his grief. Others are imagining something much more sinister."

Gabriele's heart skipped a beat. "What was the guy's name, the one who disappeared?"

"Mick Leatherby."

Gabriele exhaled. It wasn't her Lennon.

"I never met the bloke myself," Ciara continued while drying a beer mug by hand. "It all happened just before I came to town, so the news was big then. Only the twin brother left now. Apparently their mum died in childbirth."

Twin?

"What's the brother's name?"

"Callum."

Gabriele's breath hitched. A coincidence, that was all. Callum was a common name in these parts, wasn't it? She dug up her phone, pawing at it until she pulled up the photo she'd taken of Lennon the day before he died. The one that made him so angry.

"Is this... Mick?"

Ciara squinted. "Could be. Could be an old picture of Callum. That's what he looked like before he joined the army. He came in here a couple of times before he left." She studied Gabriele with narrowed eyes. "How did you get that?"

Gabriele swiveled back to look at Clover Swift. She had been Lennon's girlfriend? She was slender with platinum blond hair, the same hair colour and style Gabriele used to have.

Suddenly she felt sick to her stomach.

"Are you all right?" Ciara asked. "You don't look well." She pointed. "The loo's down the hall. Turn left by the entrance."

Gabriele threw a bunch of bills on the counter and grabbed her purse. "Thanks, Ciara."

"Sure. Come 'round again."

Gabriele just wanted to go home, crawl into bed and suffocate herself with the pillow. She pushed through the door, turned around the corner and ran smack into a hard muscular body.

Blue coat. Black cap. Sunglasses. The disguise helped to conceal his identity, but she knew who he was.

Her stalker Callum Jones.

Or should she say Callum Leatherby.

He lowered his glasses and stared down at her. With Lennon's face. Lennon's beautiful face.

Grief sprung suddenly, tearing and ripping, like loose seams pulled apart thread by thread. The sob exploded from a deep place and she couldn't stop herself from throwing herself at him. She wrapped her arms around his waist and heaved into his chest. For this moment, this one sliver of time, she let herself believe it was Lennon. That he was alive and had come back for her.

Callum's arms stayed resolutely by his side, his stiff stance reminding her, confirming to her, that this body, this face, didn't belong to Lennon.

Didn't belong to her.

She pulled back awash with embarrassment.

"Forgive me." She pushed past him, digging for a tissue to mop her face.

She heard his heavy footsteps follow from behind.

"I know my way home," she said, really wanting to be alone.

"It's my way home, too."

They walked in silence, except for the call of the birds yet to head south for the winter, down the narrow road that led to the cottage and the house. Gabriele put a hand up when Callum began to follow her down the path to her front door. "I can manage from here."

"I'm going to walk you to your door if you don't mind."

"I do mind."

"I'm going to walk you even if you do mind."

Gabriele huffed, unsure of how to manage the bundle of emotions swirling in her, including exasperation and a rapidly growing dislike for the brother of the only man she ever loved.

She thought for a second that he was going to follow her inside, but he stopped a metre away. She glanced back, amazed at how Callum's face caused her so much pain.

"I'll see you in the morning, 8 a.m. sharp," he said.

"Why?"

"I'm taking you to the airport, remember? Be ready. And don't try to dodge me again." He disappeared into the trees, and she seethed.

A new determination hammered a stake into the ground. She wasn't leaving without getting answers to her questions about Lennon. She had to learn everything she could about him. What were his parents like? What was his childhood with Callum like? Who exactly was Clover Swift and did she grieve over Lennon the way Gabriele did?

Why did Lennon change his name?

Why didn't he tell her about his girlfriend?

Gabriele set her alarm for 07:00. She would disappear somewhere in this tiny town before Callum Jones, aka Callum Leatherby swooped in to ship her away.

SLEEP WON'T COME

Then...

Gabriele moved back into the Baumann flat two weeks after Lennon died. Her mama had encouraged her to come back. "It's not good for you to be alone with only memories."

And even though her boss had said she'd hold Gabriele's job for a month, which was now up, Gabriele could only commit to part-time work. She still felt too fragile to engage with the public for more than a few hours a week, which meant she couldn't keep her flat on her own and she had to accept her parents' invitation to return to her childhood home.

She spent most of her time in her bedroom lying on her narrow bed, staring at the ceiling while holding a cushion to her stomach. It was a revised version of the fetal position, but since she now shared this space with her sister, she didn't want to be caught in obvious mourning.

Mourning was a private affair. People didn't want to witness her grief. Lennon had only been gone for four weeks, but they had already moved on. The living have to keep on living and all that.

She went through the motions of recovering to ease their discomfort, but her pain settled in like a wild furry creature hibernating through the winter. It wasn't easily seen on the surface, but it was there. A quiet angry bear.

Her mama knocked before poking her head in. "How are you, today, *Schatze?*"

Gabriele mumbled, "I'm fine."

Mama sat on the edge of her bed and took her hand. "Let me pray for you."

Gabriele tensed. Her mama came in every day to pray. What good did it do? No prayer large enough could bring Lennon back. No amount of sermonizing would explain why God had taken him away. A stupid, senseless shooting. The police couldn't, or wouldn't, say who the shooter was. Was it a random robbery? Or a case of mistaken identity?

Something more sinister?

Regardless, no perpetrator had been apprehended.

A bitter taste coated the back of her throat. How could Lennon be taken and no one held to account? Where was the justice?

She pulled her hand free. "I'd rather you not."

"Gabi."

"Please, Mama. I think God has done enough. Or not

enough. I really don't think he cares."

Her mama's eyes welled up again. One of a thousand times she'd shed tears and shared in her daughter's pain. "Of course he does."

"Please, Mama. Just let me be. I'll be fine eventually, okay? I just need more time."

Like eternity.

Mama stood and stared at her with uncertainty. Gabriele sat up and reached for the guitar on the stand by her bed. Her mama's concern softened a little. Music was therapy in her eyes. She listened to Gabriele play for a few minutes, smiled weakly and left the room.

Gabriele continued to play. Her guitar was the only thing that brought her a measure of solace. The calluses on her fingers had thickened over the last weeks as she played often, sometimes for hours at a time.

She never sang along. She couldn't stand to sing a happy song. She couldn't bear to sing a sad one. She could only hope to lose herself in the melody.

The door swung open without an introductory knock and Eva hobbled in, dropping her book bag on the floor before flopping on her bed. She always came home with the same dramatic flair. Drop the bag, sigh, flop on the bed.

Gabriele eyed her over her guitar. "Bad day?"

It was an unfair question. Eva could never have a day as bad as the one Gabriele relived every single moment. Even Eva's accident from five and a half years earlier couldn't compare to this. Death was so final.

She moaned. "Too much homework."

"Yeah, getting an education is a hardship."

Eva cut her a look. "I'm not ungrateful. It's just hard sometimes." She pushed herself up to a sitting position and leaned against her larger pillows along the wall. She tilted her head towards Gabriele. "Sebastian and I are going to hang out at Blue Note tonight. Do you want to come?"

"*No.* I don't want to be your third wheel." Gabriele couldn't believe Eva would ask. They were a couple. She was *no longer* a couple.

Eva blinked hard. "You wouldn't be our third wheel. I just thought you'd like to get out of the flat." She pulled out her phone and started texting someone. Probably Sebastian or one of her friends from the university. Her mouth pulled up in a smile at whatever she was reading and Gabriele was forgotten.

Gabriele huffed. How had this happened? Last year Eva was the girl who never left her room, who moped about without any friends, who didn't have a boyfriend or a life.

Now it was Gabriele in that position and Eva was the happy, outgoing one. The world was upside down, inside out, and every shade of blue.

Gabriele leaned back and covered her face with a pillow. It was all so impossible, so aggravating, so infuriating. If Eva wasn't in the room, she would scream.

IN SPITE OF US

Gabriele's eyes sprung open at 06:30. She dreamed of Lennon in the night, a common occurrence, only this time Callum was present, too. At times they were the same person. Her make-out dreams with Lennon were sometimes sweet, sometimes intense, and always heartbreaking when her eyes flitted open and the awful truth washed over her and she found herself in bed alone.

But last night—she groaned and whispered an apology—her kissing session had started out with Lennon, but then he morphed into his brother, his body no longer lean, but built, his hair no longer long, but combed back and short over his ears.

The lips were the same.

Oh, God. She felt like such a traitor, a cheat.

It was only a dream, but it felt so real, like she had actually made out with Callum Jones, aka Callum Leatherby.

Ack.

She had to get out of the cottage and fast. No way did she want to see Callum now. Not only did she not want to be bodily removed from the country against her will, she was also mortified that she might *blush*.

Gabriele changed into her yoga pants, a sports bra and T-shirt, and a windbreaker. What she needed was a mind-cleansing jog along the promenade and then a coffee. She approached the old, brick, A-frame building at the base of the promenade and paused to read the sign. What was now a boat club was once the town mill. The tide had been harnessed to turn the wheel that ground the grain.

Gabriele broke into an easy run and breathed deeply the saltine air. She focused on the beauty that surrounded her—the pink glow of the sunrise on the sea, the squawking of seabirds, the soothing rhythm of the channel waves. She assumed the promenade went somewhere since she'd watched people walk out of sight and not return back the way they came. She was right. It gave way to an adjoining neighborhood. She followed the road along the pond back to the main road where she took a right turn back into town. The whole time she worked to push the dream out of her mind, but it was insistent on replaying. She never kissed Callum Jones. It was only a dream. And one that would never become a reality. Callum was arrogant and heartless.

He was probably watching her cottage right now, rubbing his palms together in anticipation of kicking her out of town. She didn't understand why he was so determined to be rid of her. Why he didn't like her.

It didn't matter. She didn't like him either. She smirked, wishing she could see his face when he discovered she went

HEART & SOUL

AWOL again. She had no doubt that Callum would search for her when he discovered she was missing. The question was why? Why did Callum want her gone so badly? What was the big mystery?

Gabriele was bound and determined to get to the bottom of things, one way or another, and she didn't care how long it took. She wasn't leaving until she knew everything there was to know about her deceased husband, if it meant turning over every single rock in town to do it.

She entered the town center on the opposite side of the meridian where she usually did, turned toward the Greenhouse Cafe shop.

It was set back from the road and looked more like a little brick church with a steep roof and a steeple. The gate opened to a long, narrow area with outdoor seating, round green tables and chairs with colourful, welcoming table covers.

Gabriele approached cautiously and peeked through the windows, scanning the customers to make sure Callum wasn't there already looking for her.

Coast was clear. Gabriele entered and stood in queue, keeping her head low. She wasn't quite sure what she was worried about. It wasn't like Callum would make a scene in public, dragging her out like some cave woman, right? In fact, she had yet to see him actually *in* public. Whenever she had spotted him, he was always loitering with a cap and glasses on like he didn't want to be recognized.

What or whom was *he* hiding from?

She let out a breath. At least that meant if she wanted to stay clear of Callum, all she had to do was stay in town.

Not something she could do one hundred percent of the time, and living right next door to him was a definite liability.

Maybe she should buy a bat? Callum looked strong and fit and she doubted she'd have a chance beating him back physically. Perhaps pepper spray? She wondered where she could buy that in a quaint, family-friendly, tourist destination like Emsworth?

Gabriele's attention was attracted by the bell chiming over the door. She glanced over her shoulder and stiffened at the sight of the blond girl who entered. Clover Swift. Gabriele stared straight ahead, eyes wide and mind reeling. Less than a metre away was the girl who'd known Lennon Smith as Mick Leatherby. She'd been his girlfriend for five years, whereas Gabriele had only been with him for a total of fifteen months.

She pretended to drop something so she could swivel slightly and have another look. Clover Swift was pretty. She had a friendly face, already smiling and waving at people she knew seated at a table in the corner. They waved back with matching smiles, so it was obvious that she was well-liked.

Why would Lennon leave a girl like that? And why did he feel like he couldn't tell Gabriele about her?

Gabriele ordered a bottle of water and a cup of coffee, extra foam. She grabbed an empty table by the door and watched Clover from behind, fixated. The way she tucked her short, blond locks behind her ears, her weight on her right leg, left hip up. She ordered tea—a true Brit—with a lovely accent that was so much like Lennon's it hurt Gabriele to listen.

Gabriele ducked her head low as Clover left the shop. Without thinking it through, Gabriele jumped up after her. She walked quickly along the pavement until she reached Clover, speeding up a little more to pass her, and then purposefully knocking into her right arm, causing her tea to slosh and spill.

"I'm so sorry," Gabriele said, taking in Clover's startled expression. "My mind was in another place."

"It's okay." Clover brushed at a spot on her jeans. "Most of it spilled on the pavement."

"I'll buy you another."

"That's not necessary. I still have half a cup."

Gabriele knew she had to say something before Clover sidestepped around her and walked away. "Hey, didn't I see you at Callahans?"

Clover paused and stared at Gabriele's face. Her eyes didn't flicker with recognition.

"I'm sorry. I don't recall seeing you," she said. "Are you visiting?"

What was her story? Gabriele hadn't had a chance to weave one. "Well, I'm staying at a cottage on the beach off Tower Court. It's lovely. Red brick with white trim around the windows and doors. Tucked in beside a grove of trees. Do you know it?"

Colour visibly drained from Clover's face. "You're staying in the Leatherby cottage?"

"Yes. I'm… family."

Clover blinked. "You sound like you're German."

"Yes, well, we're distant family. Did you know the Leatherbys?"

"Excuse me, but I don't think I caught your name?"

"Gabriele Baumann." She left the name Smith off, since it obviously wasn't a German name and she didn't want Clover to ask any more questions.

"I'm trying to locate Mick Leatherby," Gabriele continued.

The name stuck in her throat, but she forced herself to say it. It was Lennon's real name after all.

"That's a name I haven't heard in ages." Clover ducked her head. "Did you know Mick?"

What a loaded question. *Well, I was married to him, but his name wasn't Mick.*

Gabriele swallowed. "Not well. Did you?"

Clover huffed. "Yeah. I was his girlfriend. The damn bloke just took off, no word of explanation." Her eyes grew glassy. "I think something horrible happened to him, but no one will talk. Not even his brother."

"When was the last time you saw him?"

"At the uni, almost three years ago. We met for lunch in the cafeteria. I knew something was wrong. He looked a little dicky."

"Dicky?"

"Sick. I even asked him if he was coming down with something. He said no, then we snogged. It was a good, proper snog, you know." She smiled weakly. Gabriele felt her cheeks redden at the thought of Lennon kissing another girl, but she just nodded, encouraging Clover to continue.

"He didn't show up for uni the next day. Didn't answer his mobile or respond to texts. I thought maybe he was having a breakdown after losing his dad. He grew up without a mum, so he and his brother were orphans. But then all his social media disappeared." She sniffed. "That's when I knew he didn't want me to find him."

She stared at Gabriele with watery eyes. "I don't know why I'm telling you this."

Gabriele's heart hurt for the girl. They were both

brokenhearted over the same boy.

"It's a mystery I'm sure had nothing to do with you." She said that to comfort Clover, but Gabriele thought it must be the truth. She couldn't imagine Lennon behaving in such a thoughtless way.

A tug on her arm made her swirl around and she groaned. Caught.

She heard Clover's voice. "Callum?"

He looked up and grunted, but forced a smile. "Hi, Clover."

His eyes cut to Gabriele and his smile disappeared.

"I thought you were in, like, overseas or something," Clover said.

"No, just London."

"Oh, I haven't seen you around, so I just assumed." She motioned to Gabriele. "Your cousin and I were just having a nice chat."

A muscle in Callum's jaw twitched. "I see. My *cousin* has a plane to catch. It was nice to see you again, Clover."

Clover stared hard at Callum, a fleet of emotions flashing behind hazel eyes. Gabriele recognized this look. She suffered from the same things when she was in close quarters with Callum: sorrow, confusion... and attraction.

They said awkward good-byes and Clover turned the corner continuing on to wherever she was going. Callum pushed Gabriele's elbow to guide her across the meridian.

She tugged her arm away. "Don't touch me." Gabriele refused to be bullied or manipulated. She scrambled down High Street away from Callum.

He snorted but stayed on her heels. He put on his dark sunglasses and pulled his dark wool cap on his head.

"Not a great disguise," Gabriele muttered.

He kept his head low. "It's the best I can do under the circumstances."

"Under *what* circumstances?"

He ignored her question. "You weren't ready for me this morning."

"Charming and bright."

"Shall we try again?"

Gabriele spun and stared up at his face, seeing Callum and not Lennon for the first time. "I have every legal right to stay in that cottage as long as I want. It's *mine*. Lennon left it to *me*. Perhaps you're mad he didn't leave it to you, but too bad. Now back off!"

She thought she'd shaken him when she didn't immediately hear his heavy steps behind her, but she should've known better. Callum Leatherby-Jones was a bulldog with a bone when it came to getting her to leave town. He jogged up beside her.

They walked in emotionally charged silence past the Irish pub and down toward the shore. Gabriele paused for a second. Was it safe to go back with Callum on her heels? How far was he willing to go to get rid of her? At least Clover Swift knew she was staying there and she'd seen Callum. She had a witness.

Of course, Lennon had disappeared without a trace.

"Look," Callum finally said, "Let's call a truce."

"Sure. I go to my home and you go to yours and we never see each other again."

"I was thinking more like dinner."

"I'm thinking, hell no."

"At my house. You can look through the family photo albums."

Gabriele stopped short. "Your house? You own it?"

"I inherited it when my dad died. It's where Mick and I grew up. I'm sure you're curious."

Understatement of the year.

She didn't look at him when she asked, "What time?"

"Seven o'clock."

"Fine."

She resisted the urge to glance back at him, though she felt him watching her. He didn't disappear through the trees on the property-line until she was inside.

WAKE ME UP IN SUMMERTIME

Then...

New buds on dew-covered trees, rising birdsong, shoots of green forcing up from cold, hardened ground: it was the battle between seasons. Winter not wanting to let go of its frozen kingdom, spring not giving up until it did.

It was a reflection of Gabriele's heart. It was cold and despondent, clinging to the frosty bitterness and crisp sadness. Every once in a while Gabriele's spirit would rise with a memory that made her smile, or a surprising if subtle bout of laughter, just to be plunged once again into dark murky water.

Her grief was unpredictable, at times unmanageable, and could not be scheduled. She'd spent more than one night curled up on the bathroom floor, weeping into a towel so as not to wake Eva or her parents.

She did her best to keep evidence of it at bay. She thought she was succeeding until her boss called her in to her office one day.

The woman told her to have a seat and took the chair with wheels behind an uncluttered desk. Her hair was gray and short curls framed her face. "Gabriele," she said kindly, "I know this is a hard time for you, and I'm not placating. I lost my first husband as a young bride myself, so believe me, I *know*.

"However, we've been receiving unflattering comments about your work here, which need to be addressed."

Gabriele's chest tightened. "I've been working hard."

"That's not what is causing me concern. It's the quality of your presentations. They are without enthusiasm. It's as if you've memorized a script and recite it like a robot. Tourists, our clients, want to engage with our guides. Be entertained, if you will."

She leaned forward, rested her arms flat on her desk and looked Gabriele in the eye. "At the very least, you need to smile."

"You're right, Frau Messer." Gabriele forced the requested smile. "I will endeavor to do better."

Her boss leaned back and smiled in return. "That's all I ask."

Gabriele rode her bike home, allowing the tears to fall. She could blame them on the wind in her eyes, or the sun that peeked through thinning clouds.

Once home, she hid away in her room, ignoring her

mama's knock, pretending to be napping when she inched the door open to look inside.

Frau Messer had gone through this. Many women have. Somehow Gabriele would too. She had to. She couldn't imagine living the rest of her life in this heavy state of melancholy. It was like she was experiencing life while trapped inside a transparent cocoon. She could see people engaging all around her, but she was helpless to participate.

She was just so tired. Every single cell in her body was exhausted. Her mind and spirit were tremendously fatigued as well. She wished she could sleep until this was over.

Her guitar was her friend. It understood. She played it, and the words expressing her feelings flooded onto the page of her notebook. For the first time since Lennon left, she sang.

Wake me up in Summer Time
The air is cold
Don't wanna go
Just stay in bed, where it's warm
The nights are long
And sleep won't come
Dreamin' awake of the sun

Wake me up in Summer time
The warmth seeps in the layers of my skin
Wake me up in Summer time
Leave me buried in these blankets to my chin.

SECRETS AND SCARE TACTICS

Gabriele paced the small cabin, snorting and fuming. That man! He'd manipulated her with the promise of something he knew she couldn't say no to. Fine. She'd see the photo albums at least. Maybe be the one to manipulate him into giving up answers.

She collapsed on the sofa and punched the pillow. She wished she knew why they were at war. But he'd started it.

Gabriele needed to calm down. She hated how Callum had gotten under her skin so quickly. She wasn't going to give him this kind of power. Wasn't going to let him ruin what was promising to be a beautiful fall day.

Her stomach growled and now she wished she would've ordered from the cafe's all-day breakfast menu. She had eggs in the fridge that she'd purchased the day before. She went to work scrambling a few and popped two questionable pieces of fluffy bread into the toaster.

She felt better after she ate. She had a shower. Played the guitar. Went for a walk towards the east end of the quay.

Later she read a book as she sipped coffee on her terrace. Her eyes kept darting to the higher windows on the house next door. How vain of her to think Callum loitered up there just to watch her.

She continuously checked the time, waiting for the hour she knew that Julia would be returning home from work. She dialed her friend's number and held her phone to her ear. "He has a brother."

A pause on the other end, then, "Oh my God, Gabi. Seriously?"

"Seriously. And an old girlfriend."

"Wait. I think I need a drink. No, keep talking. I'll pour while you spill."

Gabriele made her way back inside to her bedroom and flopped on the bed. If Callum was watching her, she didn't want him witnessing this call. With her luck, he could read lips. "The brother inherited the house next door." She sighed. "He's quite eager for me to leave."

Gabriele could hear Julia clanging about in her kitchen. "Why?" she asked. "Did he not know about you, either?"

"Yeah, he knew. He and Lennon kept in touch."

"But why didn't Lennon tell you about him?"

Gabriele rubbed the frown lines on her forehead "I don't know."

"This is crazy. Have you told your family?"

"No. I want to do it in person when I get home."

"Naturally. But, wow... Does he look like Lennon?"

Gabriele hedged. "A little."

"That must me so weird for you. Are you all right? It's not tossing you off the deep end, is it?"

"I'm fine."

"Really? You don't sound fine."

"I am. I promise."

"When are you coming home?"

"I don't know. It depends."

"Depends on what?"

"Just depends, Julia."

"Do you want me to come there? I could take a sick day."

"It's all right. I'll be coming home soon anyway. Selling is sounding like a good idea right about now."

"Okay. So what are you doing tonight? Do you have TV?"

Gabriele hesitated before answering. "I'm going to Callum's for dinner."

"Who's Callum?"

"That's Lennon's brother."

"You're DATING Lennon's brother?"

"NO. For goodness sake, Julia. I'm searching for answers. He said I could look through photo albums."

"And to do this you must eat dinner with him?"

"Yes. And promise that I'll be on the first flight out tomorrow morning."

"Make sure you take a picture. I can't wait to see what he looks like. And see if you can sneak one of the girlfriend—did you meet her?"

Gabriele could picture her friend with wide, curious eyes, holding a glass of wine in one hand as she held her phone to her ear with the other.

"Yes," Gabriele answered.

"That must've been so weird!"

"It was."

"And Lennon never mentioned her?"

"Nope."

"Oh Gabi. I'm so sorry for you. Like you haven't had enough shock in your life."

"I'll be okay. But I should go. I have to make myself presentable."

"Okay. I can't wait until you get back. You have to tell me *everything*!"

At fifteen minutes to the hour Gabriele was ready. Showered, hair washed and blown-dry. Jeans that fit her curves, a form-fitting blouse. Makeup.

It wasn't a date, but that didn't mean she didn't want to make him wish it were one. It was the only leverage she had. She silently apologized to Lennon.

She left for the house next door five minutes late, not wanting to appear too eager. Her hands tingled with nerves and she wiped the dampness off on her thighs before knocking.

The door immediately swung open.

"You're late."

His face still shocked her, and she wondered if she'd ever get used to seeing Lennon's likeness. She quickly averted her eyes, shrugging with a pretense of not being perturbed and pushed past him. "Five minutes."

"I thought Germans loved precision."

"I thought Brits were friendlier."

Callum didn't even crack a smile to prove her wrong. It was going to be an interesting dinner.

The main entrance opened up into a foyer with hooks on the wall for jackets and a bench for sitting on while you tied up your shoes. There were no jackets or shoes. Gabriele wore a cardigan and kept both it and her shoes on.

The entrance opened up to a hallway with several doors. The house was large and boxy inside, with the living room, dining room and kitchen all separated from each other. She followed Callum into the living room. A fan hung from a high ceiling, not in use in the cooler fall weather. The walls were covered in old, worn-looking wallpaper. A bookshelf covered one wall, an older television in the middle of it and a brick fireplace built into the corner. The furniture was old and well-used.

Gabriele waved a hand. "I expected something…"

"Else? Not old widower chic?"

"Yeah, more younger guy." Something that would tell her what Callum was really like. Except for his near identical physical appearance to Lennon, she couldn't figure him out. She examined the room as he watched her with a mixture of intrigue, amusement in his eyes. And something darker.

He didn't like her. Obviously.

This was clear not only by his poorly suppressed scowl, but by the way he'd been trying to chase her away.

The question was why. She'd given him no reason to dislike her, and she'd been a perfect neighbour in the short time she'd been here. The answer lay with Lennon, and Callum was being stubbornly tight-lipped about what he knew.

Hanging on one of the walls was a collection of two-photos-in-one-frame pictures of the Leatherby brothers at different stages of life. Toddlers, early school years, teen years. They were always dressed the same with matching haircuts until the teen photos when it was apparent they were trying to individuate from each other. Gabriele had known Lennon well enough to pick out which child was him in each pairing.

She stroked the latest picture.

Callum stepped in beside her. "That was year thirteen of school."

"What was it like growing up as identical twins?"

Callum shrugged and folded his arms.

"I mean, I have a sister, but she's younger than me and except for our eyes, we don't look much alike. We never had the same friends or really hung out that much growing up."

"Being together all the time and sharing everything was all Mick and I knew. When we were younger it made us feel special. We were unique. As we got older, we started to resent it. Me more than Mick, I think. We drifted apart. Getting mistaken for someone else by people you've known all your life gets old."

Gabriele hadn't thought about it before, but now that she considered Callum's words, she didn't think she'd do very well as an identical twin to someone else. She and Eva were very different and Gabriele was glad of it.

Callum hadn't shifted away and Gabriele was keenly aware of his nearness. She missed having a man in her life. She missed Lennon.

But his brother was creating a physical awareness that warmed her. She could feel him looking at her and she risked a glance. His eyes were dark, intense pools of emotion and not necessarily pleasant ones. She took a small step back and removed her cardigan.

"Whatever you're cooking smells good," she said to break the spell.

"It's takeout."

"You could've faked it and impressed me."

"That would be lying."

She scoffed. "Something I don't think you have a problem with."

He narrowed his gaze at her, but didn't deny it.

"Where are those photo albums you promised?"

Callum pointed to the bottom shelf of the bookcase and waved. "Help yourself."

Gabriele pulled the first in the row, an old style photo album with a fat wire ring binding with half the fabric worn off. Here was an album that had been opened many times. She settled onto the carpeted floor, crossed her legs and flipped the cover.

The first pictures were vintage-style photos of a happy couple, arm in arm. The young woman had big 80s hair with poofy bangs and the man wore a mullet, short on top and long at the back. Despite the hair, Gabriele could see that they were a good-looking couple and that by the way they smiled and stared at each other, they seemed to be in love.

"Your parents." It was a statement rather than a question. Her *parents-in law*.

"Yeah. I don't remember my mother. She died shortly after I was born."

"You mean when Lennon was born. He came second, right?"

"She was already dead when they pulled him from her

body."

"Oh." A deep sadness, deeper than her own, swirled in her heart. "That's terrible."

"Dad did a good job raising us. We lived like a bunch of bachelors, no homemade bread or sweets, but Dad put the effort in to cook for us. He put us in football and kept this roof over our heads."

"It's a nice roof," Gabriele said. Even with the tired interior, a big house on the beach like this would be worth something. She knew how much the cottage would sell for, an amount that made her blush.

She caught his gaze. "How did your dad die?"

Callum's eyes flickered like he was calculating. "A heart attack."

It was what Lennon had told her, but the way Callum had answered, it made her believe it wasn't true. But why would they lie about that?

She was getting paranoid.

Gabriele flipped through pages of print photographs of the boys: playing on the beach, opening presents under a Christmas tree, playing football—standing with their team, white balls underfoot and medals around their necks. Her heart pinged at every clip of Lennon, and then did a dizzying dip when she came to one where he had an arm around a cute little blond girl.

"That's Clover?"

Callum squatted and leaned close over her shoulder. She could smell his aftershave. It was muskier than what Lennon wore, and she was glad he didn't smell the same. Still, he smelled good and her heart sped up in a very disconcerting manner. She swallowed hard and focused on the picture of the girl.

"Yes. That was the day of our sixteenth birthday party."

HEART & SOUL

Dad always threw us a big bar-b-que. It became a tradition.

Gabriele's heart squeezed as she flipped through more pages of pictures of Lennon and Clover together. She was obviously a big part of his life.

She sighed. "He never mentioned her."

There were pictures of Callum with girls, too. Always a different one. Another way the brothers were different. Lennon was loyal.

Until he wasn't.

She slapped the albums shut, and loaded them back onto the shelf. She didn't know what she hoped to find, how she thought she would feel while seeing Lennon's past. Her heart felt hollow.

"You look like you could use a glass of wine."

Gabriele had been so consumed with the images of Lennon and Clover, she hadn't even noticed that Callum had slipped away. He handed her a goblet of red wine. She took it without saying thanks, concluding he knew she drank red and not white in the same way he knew how she took her coffee and played guitar.

Lennon must have told him.

"Why did your brother tell you about me, but he never mentioned one word about you?"

Callum leaned against the door frame that led to the dining room. His shoulders stiffened and a shadow crossed his face. "I wish you could ask him that yourself."

"I wish I could too, but clearly I can't. Why don't you just tell me?"

He eyed her, and for a moment she thought he was going to tell her. Then he said, "We should eat."

Callum turned and left her feeling frustrated and helpless.

Fine. He wouldn't answer her most burning questions, but that didn't mean she was done trying.

"May I use the loo?" Gabriele asked. She wanted to wash her hands before eating but she also needed a small break from Callum, a moment to get her head together.

"It's up the stairs, first door to the left."

She took her time, taking in the aged wallpaper and the markings on the wall as she went up the steps, every odd one groaning as if it couldn't bear to lift her weight. How many times had Lennon run up and down these stairs?

The dimly lit hall had a number of doors and she was instantly curious. She padded quickly by the open bathroom door wondering which closed door was Lennon's old room. She supposed she could just ask Callum, but he was so irrationally guarded about anything that had to do with his brother, she doubted if he'd be agreeable. All she wanted was a quick look. Maybe she'd see something that would shed a light on what has become a huge mystery. She pressed her fingertips against the first door, hoping it would slide open, but it was firmly shut. She slowly pushed the handle down and it clicked open.

Just a quick peek.

It opened to a bedroom, but the bedsheets were mussed and clothes were strewn over a chair. This wasn't Lennon's abandoned bedroom. Clearly occupied, it must belong to Callum. She stepped back, feeling like she just crossed a line into his personal space and had started closing the door when her eyes landed on a set of small binoculars on a table by the window. A dark cloud filled her chest, and even though she instinctively knew what the view was beyond, she had to see it for herself. She skipped across the room to the window, pushed back the net curtains and swallowed. A perfect view of her terrace.

She hadn't imagined it. He was peeping on her!

Why?

Her eyes darted around the room. She didn't know what she was looking for, anything to explain what was going on. His dresser top was clear except for a few sundry items: a brush, cologne, a tie curled up like a snake in a basket. One of the smaller drawers near the top was opened a crack. Gabriele peeked inside. She eased the drawer open carefully and frowned. Passports for three different countries, none of them England.

Who did they belong to?

Before she could take a look, her attention snapped aware to the creaking of the stairs. She darted out of the room and gently closed the door just as Callum topped the stairs. His eyes narrowed. "Gabriele?"

"Sorry, I got a little disoriented." She faked an embarrassed smile. "Silly me."

He pinned her to the wall with a suspicious glare. She forced herself to stand tall and walk by him back down the stairs.

"You don't mind if we eat in the kitchen?" Callum asked stiffly as he followed her from behind.

"Not at all." She stopped to let him pass. The hallway was narrow and he took his time inching by her, head bent as he stared down hard. She carefully kept her eyes averted, fully aware of the heat coming from his strong, hard body. He knew she'd been snooping. She waited for him to accuse her, but since he hadn't actually seen her leave his room, it was speculation on his part. An accusation would be rude and would definitely bring an end to their evening. She let out a slow breath when he finally led her to the kitchen without saying another word.

Gabriele had spotted a larger, formal room for eating earlier, but guessed that Callum only ever ate here. The table was smaller, but the room overall was much cozier.

Callum removed an aluminum pan from the oven. He dished out mounds of rice on two plates, then spooned on an orange sauce. "It's chicken curry."

Gabriele pulled back one of the chairs and sat. "I love Indian food."

There was a small, well-used candle on the table and Gabriele was relieved that Callum didn't light it. That would've made it too much like a date. There was music playing in the background, low and not what she would consider romantic. She took another long breath and tried to relax.

"So you got the big house and Lennon got the cottage," she said. "How come?"

"I'm twelve minutes older. Funny thing is, Lennon was fine with the split. I don't think I would've been if the situation were reversed."

Gabriele didn't find that hard to believe. She took another sip of her wine.

"You're prettier in real life than in your pictures," Callum surprised her by saying. "And your pictures were hot."

Gabriele's eyelashes fluttered and her neck warmed with embarrassment. "Lennon sent you pictures of me?" Lennon didn't have a Facebook page. He wasn't a fan of any kind of social media site so Callum wouldn't have stumbled upon pictures.

Callum sipped his wine in response. He gazed at her over the rim of his glass. "I like your hair better this way. Dark suits you."

Gabriele's stomach clenched. "Is that why Lennon pursued me? Because of my *hair*? Was he looking for another Clover?"

"Your hairstyle and your resemblance to Clover may have been what first caught his eye, but..." He shot her a sly grin. "He never married Clover."

No, he didn't. The question was *why?* Was Clover the reason he left England? If so, she wasn't aware of it. Unless she was lying? Maybe it was just a cover story and Clover really did know.

"Did you go to the same uni as Lennon?"

"For a while."

"You didn't finish?"

"I joined the army. I finished there."

"Why'd you join the army?"

Callum's fork paused midair. "It seemed like the right thing to do at the time."

"What time?"

Callum's face twitched like he was holding back a scowl. "I work as a civil servant," he said, avoiding the question. "City planning, working to make the city of London more sustainable." He eyed her. "How about you? Did you finish uni?"

Gabriele snorted. "I'm assuming that you already know the answer to that question."

"Why'd you assume that?"

"Because you already know how I like my coffee and that I play guitar." She lifted her glass. "That I prefer red wine to white."

Callum answered by stuffing more food in his mouth.

"If you and Lennon weren't estranged, which obviously you weren't since you were still in contact, why didn't he tell me about you? Seriously, why?"

"Your English is very good."

"Stop changing the subject!"

"I'm just saying."

"I majored in English. I speak five languages fluently and am trained as a translator."

"Hmm."

"Hmm, what?"

"That's interesting."

Gabriele snorted. "I'm so glad to be able to entertain you."

"I don't want you to entertain me. I want you to listen to me."

"Listen or obey?"

"Both."

"Too bad."

"Okay, I'll settle for listen. There was a reason Mick had to leave, a reason he didn't tell you about me. I can't tell you why, but you being here is dangerous."

"*Dangerous?*" She stifled a nervous laugh. "How so?"

"I can't tell you. It just is. And it's in everyone's best interest if you leave immediately."

Gabriele dropped her fork and laughed. "You're incredible, you know that? All secrets and scare tactics. Emsworth is the least dangerous place on the planet." She stood sharply and threw her serviette on the table. "Do you want the cottage? Is that what this is about? You know, if you had been nicer to me, I might have considered a deal. But now, I'll sell to anyone but you. And that's if I sell."

She didn't wait for Callum to see her out or walk her home,

HEART&SOUL

and for a change he didn't follow her, but she glanced up at the second-story window on the roadside of the house when she got to her front door and saw the outline of his silhouette watching her.

HOLES IN THE NIGHTSKY

Gabriele was too agitated to sit and far too aggravated to sleep. Television served as a temporary distraction. Even playing the guitar Callum had left for her failed to soothe her nerves. The instrument itself was a reminder of his egotistical, big-headedness. He was trying to strong arm her and Gabriele wasn't about to be wrestled down by the likes of him.

How could she feel so furious and indignant towards one brother and so tender and heartbroken over the other? The familiar ache that had taken up residence in her chest was now bound with something else. The deep ache of extreme loss mixed with the twisty kind of hot angry pain that comes from feeling duped.

Lennon Smith wasn't Lennon Smith. He was Mick Leatherby, the boy who became a man just one property over. The boy who became a man playing on this very beach, celebrating a shared birthday with his twin at an annual bar-b-que hosted by their single father.

The boy who had a life in England he'd chosen not to share with her.

A sob erupted in her chest, and a burning tore through her throat as she fought to push it back down.

Enough! She swiped her sleeve under her nose and pressed the cuffs of her blouse against her tear ducts. She'd shed enough tears for Lennon Smith and she wasn't going to shed one more. She pulled out her phone and removed Smith from her last name on all her social sites. She couldn't even be sure her marriage had been legal. She took off her ring.

Gabriele released a loud moan into the semi darkness. So much pain! How could Lennon do this to her?

Why did he have to lie?

Why did he have to *die?*

She couldn't stay here. She needed out. Needed air. She quickly freshened up, doing a half-baked job with her makeup which surprisingly she didn't care about, grabbed her coat and purse and left for the pub. According to the sign on the street, it was open mic night. She was ready to see what kind of talent this town had to offer.

Gabriele had traveled this path from the cottage to the town so many times in the last few days she could almost do it with her eyes closed. Which was a good thing. A cloud covering blanketed the moon and it was almost pitch black. At least she had a torch app on her phone.

She walked with determination, the crunch of her footsteps and the sound of her breath in her ears.

A branch snapping?

Gabriele swiveled around. She aimed her light in a circle around her, but its rays didn't go far and she couldn't see around the soft bend of the narrow alley.

"Callum?" she spoke out cautiously. It wouldn't surprise her one bit if he was following her. "Don't be an idiot," she called more courageously.

No response. She was pretty sure Callum would've identified himself. He might be a jerk, but he wasn't a psycho. He wouldn't scare her intentionally.

Would he?

No, of course not.

Unless he was the reason Lennon left? Did they have a falling out? Was the danger Callum referred to Callum himself?

That was crazy. The bush behind her shifted. She shot the light of her phone to the sound. She couldn't see anyone. It was just the wind. Or maybe a squirrel.

Gabriele picked up her pace. All of Callum's spooky talk was just getting to her.

Still, she couldn't shake the feeling that she was being watched and breathed a sigh of relief when she reached the pub and opened the door to the energetic atmosphere.

Callahans buzzed with conversation competing with the Irish tunes pumping in through the sound system set up on the stage. The air was warm from crowded bodies—open mic nights were obviously popular—and smelled strongly of beer and deep-fried foods.

Ciara spotted her and waved her over to the table where she was sitting. "Push down everyone," she said. "This is Gabriele."

The group at the table acknowledged her, then went back to their conversations.

"Not working tonight?" Gabriele asked.

Ciara smiled. "My brother gives me time off to have a life."

"And yet, here you are."

"I know, right? But Callahans is the place to be on a Thursday night."

A server came over and Gabriele ordered a beer. She glanced around and the only other person she knew in the place was Clover. When their gazes connected, Clover quickly averted her eyes. The guy beside Clover put an arm around her chair. Clover shot him a look and pushed it off. The guy scowled.

Gabriele asked Ciara, "Who is that?"

Ciara followed Gabriele's gaze. "Sitting beside Clover Swift? That's Rupert Kingsley. He and Clover are a thing. More like an off again/on again thing. Looks like it might be off again."

Rupert Kingsley had a hard edge to his face with hooded eyes that stared at Clover with a dark intensity that made Gabriele uncomfortable. Gabriele couldn't help but wonder how Clover had ended up with a guy like that. Maybe she wouldn't have if Lennon had stuck around.

Riley Callahan jumped on stage and took the mic. "Welcome to open mic night at Callahans. Thanks for coming out."

Gabriele leaned into Ciara. "Your brother is cute. Does he have a girlfriend?"

She laughed. "Why, are you interested?"

Gabriele's interest was purely tabloid. The idea that she might date again was a foreign one.

Or, at least it had been.

Ciara laughed. "You look like a scared rabbit. Don't worry. I won't try to set you up if you don't want to be. Besides, he keeps claiming he's too busy to date."

"I'm sure he has his pick of girls."

"Yeah, all but the one he really wants."

"And who's that?"

"Ah, Callahans don't gossip about each other." She grinned and took a swig of her beer. Riley Callahan called up the first act. A younger guy, Gabriele guessed him to still be in his teens, jumped up with a guitar. He sang a cover tune. He wasn't great, but the crowd was friendly and shouted encouragement.

Gabriele drank her beer and tried to shake off her nerves. She was here to relax and that was exactly what she was going to do. When the server came by again, she ordered another.

She was surprised when Riley announced the next singer. "Folks, please welcome my sister, Ciara Callahan!"

Gabriele gawked as Ciara jumped up, shimmied through the crowded chairs and jumped on stage. She picked up the guitar sitting on stage and strapped it on. The crowd hooted and some shouted out requests. Evidently this wasn't the first time Ciara had played.

"Thanks, guys. Here's one I know you like."

Ciara had real talent. Her hands moved expertly along the fret of the guitar, her fingers flexible and fluid. Her voice was husky, yet crystal clear.

Gabriele applauded enthusiastically when the song ended. "You were great! Did you write that?"

Ciara nodded. "I like to dabble in songwriting."

"Me, too." Gabriele almost blurted out her claim to fame, a sister who dated a rock star, but refrained. She liked to be judged on her own merits, not based on who she knew.

Ciara nudged her. "I'd love to hear you play."

"Nah, I'm just here to listen."

"C'mon. You don't know anybody here. It's the safest place."

Gabriele knew what Ciara meant. Playing to strangers was easier in some ways than playing to people you knew. It didn't matter so much what they thought. You'd never see them again anyway.

Gabriele emptied her second pint, feeling braver. Why not? She needed something to make her feel alive again.

"Do I just storm the stage?"

Ciara laughed. "I'll tell my brother. He'll call you up next."

Gabriele watched Ciara as she made her way to where Riley stood by the bar. She pointed at Gabriele and Gabriele waved. Riley nodded his dark head and offered her a friendly smile.

Ciara returned just as the last act finished to appreciative applause. And as promised, Riley called her up.

"We have a newcomer all the way from Dresden, Germany. Please welcome Gabriele!"

A surge of adrenaline energized her and she made her way to the stage. This was just like karaoke, but with a guitar.

"I wonder if the band wouldn't mind helping me out with this one." They hopped back on stage, and she called out the timing and key.

She strapped on Ciara's guitar and ran her fingers along the strings, plucking a few notes to warm up and get a feel for the instrument.

She scanned the audience and let out a breath. Besides Ciara, Riley and Clover, she didn't know anyone. And she didn't even really know those three.

Then the door opened and a dark figure shifted into the back.

Scheisse! Why did Callum have to show up now?

Her heart stuttered and stopped. She really didn't want to play in front of him. He already knew so much about her and she had been determined that he wouldn't see anything more.

A silence descended and Gabriele could see the faces in the crowd watching with eager anticipation, wondering, no doubt, if this new girl was any good.

Her only options were to play or leave without playing. The latter would be humiliating for her and embarrassing for the Callahans. She forged ahead.

"I wrote this song for someone I loved who left me suddenly." She let her gaze settle on Callum. His eyes were dark and intense, undistracted and captivated. She counted the band in and began to play.

Looking into Vincent's starlight swirl
like portals into the spirit world
We were just hoping that someone heard
this brokenhearted boy and girl

Hold on, I'm falling for you
Inside of us, in spite of us there is a star that shines
This light in us, in spite of us, is keeping hope alive

Didn't we say that the stars were just holes in the night sky
letting the light shine in from a better world
Didn't we think that the stars were just holes in the night sky

Letting the light shine in from a better world
You are my star, letting the light shine in
From a better world

The crowd erupted when she finished and she basked in the applause. She couldn't stop herself from glancing over at

HEART & SOUL

Callum, and a smug, satisfied smile crossed her face when she saw a hint of a grin. His arms unfolded and he clapped slowly with appreciation.

Acceptance, Almost

Then...

She survived the year of firsts. First Christmas, first Valentine's Day. Her birthday, his birthday. Summertime. Their wedding day.

And now today, the last of the firsts. The anniversary of Lennon's death.

Time *did* go on as unfair as that was. The sun kept setting and rising. The seasons kept changing. People fell in and out of love. They were born and they died.

Gabriele had lived life without Lennon now for almost as long as she had lived life with him. The time they'd shared in this world had been impossibly short. If she should live to be an old lady, the Lennon Year would be just a blip on the screenplay of her life.

An intense, meaningful, beautiful, excruciating blip.

HEART&SOUL

Today was the last of the firsts and it still lay ahead of her. A glance at her phone told her it was 08:35. She didn't want to get out of bed.

Eva's bed was empty; she'd left for uni an hour earlier. Gabriele had heard her get ready, felt her hover over her. Eva knew what day this was, too, but Gabriele didn't want to face it yet. She pretended to sleep and then actually did. She dreamed of Lennon, of course. Another makeout dream. He was always kissing her and undressing her. It was the last thing they had done together when he was alive, so it didn't surprise her that this was the moment she often revisited in her dreams.

The dreams used to throw her into an emotional tizzy, the wound of his death just too raw, but now they felt more like a balm. They comforted her.

This dream was different than the others. Lennon had spoken to her. "Good-bye, Gabi," he said. "Live well." Then he disappeared like an apparition.

It made her both sad and hopeful. *Live well.* She had no idea how to do that.

A knock on the door was followed by the entrance of her mama. She had a bouquet of flowers in her hand, already placed in a water-filled vase.

"I brought these for you. To brighten your day."

"Thanks, Mama. They're beautiful."

Her mama sat on the side of the bed and reached for Gabriele's hand. "Can I pray for you?"

She hadn't asked since the last time Gabriele had turned

her away. Her mama's eyes were so full of love and compassion, and Gabriele couldn't bear to hurt her feelings by saying no. Besides, a little prayer couldn't hurt.

"Sure, Mama."

Her mama's hand was warm and soft, and her words of prayer focused heavenward were soothing and comforting. Gabriele felt her resistance fall away and she accepted the words of peace, drawing them around her like a shawl.

Her mama said, "Amen," then kissed her on the head. "I'll make breakfast."

Gabriele showered and dressed. She stared at her image in the mirror. She used to bother with her appearance, keeping regular hair and nail appointments. Her previously short, platinum bleach-blond hair had grown out over the last year. When her natural brunette roots had grown out several centimetres, Mama had presented a new box of dye to match things up.

Now her darker hair had grown past her shoulders, she rarely wore any makeup—

weeping didn't lend itself well to the practice—and she kept her nails short for the guitar.

Lennon would hardly recognize her.

She ate a small breakfast, then walked the twenty-minute trek to the graveyard where Lennon's body was buried. Her mama had offered to come along, but Gabriele reassured her that she was fine to go alone. It was what she needed.

The surrounding trees, newly turned yellow and red, dotted the grounds. Gabriele knelt on the damp moss and wiped the gravestone clean. She cried like she knew she would, but the tears came from a different place now. Sorrowful, but mixed with a small portion of acceptance.

"What now, Lennon?" she asked. "What do I do now?"

She disliked her job, but couldn't afford to leave it. She appreciated how her parents took care of her, but she was a twenty-five-year-old woman. She needed to take care of herself.

Gabriele felt stuck. Her heart had softened enough that she could manage a few short prayers of her own. There must be an answer somewhere.

And there was. It arrived at the same time Eva did.

Gabriele was sitting at the kitchen table eating a slice of marble cake her mother had made when Eva came home with a formal envelope.

"The postal worker was at the door when I got there," she said. "I signed for it."

Mama wiped damp hands on a T-towel. "Is it for Papa?"

"No." She handed it to Gabriele. "It's for you."

The cream-coloured envelope had the name of a law firm in the return address. Gabriele narrowed her eyes, confused. She'd been told that all the death registration requirements had been taken care of. She wasn't exactly clear how, just that Lennon's company had managed it.

Eva sat on a chair beside Gabriele. "Are you going to open it?"

Gabriele ran a finger under the seal and removed the documents. Strange. They were in English. She pushed back at the lump growing in her throat and read on.

"Gabi, you should see your face," Eva said. "What is it?"

Her mama stepped closer. "*Schatzi?*"

Gabriele glanced at both of them, to the papers in her hand and back again. Her eyes flickered with disbelief.

"It's Lennon's will. He left me something."

"What?" Eva demanded. "What did he leave you?"

"A cottage. In England."

STARLIGHT SWIRL

Gabriele shook hands with the band members, thanking them again. A flush of euphoria surged through her veins as she relived the last few minutes. It'd been a long time since she played in front of anyone. Once in a while Lennon would prod her to play at the Blue Note Pub in Neustadt, and they often sat in circles at the park with their friends on the weekends, passing a guitar around to those who played.

She placed the guitar in its stand and stepped off the stage just as a commotion stirred at one of the tables near the front. Gabriele focused her gaze past the house lights to the source and witnessed a verbal dispute between Clover Swift and her sometimes boyfriend Rupert Kingsley.

Clover's voice cut through the din that had suddenly quieted as the crowd observed the spectacle. "Just leave me alone!"

Rupert grabbed her wrist.

Gabriele had the perspective of the whole room. Riley took strides from the bar. Callum moved in from the door. This was a set up for a bad scene.

Gabriele's legs seemed to move on their own, and within two seconds she found herself between the squabbling affair. She extended her hand awkwardly to Rupert.

"Hi there. I'm Gabriele."

His intense eyes moved from Clover to Gabriele's hand. It was like a switch had gone off in his head and he was just now realizing that the whole room was watching him, witnessing his abuse of his girlfriend.

His gaze moved to Gabriele's face and his countenance sobered. He had to release his grip from Clover's wrist to accept Gabriele's hand. His eyes moved once more to the people watching and back to Gabriele's face. She hoped he couldn't see the fear she felt in that moment. She wasn't exactly looking to be Rupert's next target.

He begrudgingly shook her hand. Gabriele cringed inside as his large clammy palm wrapped around hers.

"Rupert," he muttered.

"Nice to meet you. I hope you enjoyed my song."

"Yeah, yeah. It was good." Rupert slunk back to his seat and took a swig from his beer like nothing had just happened.

"Clover," she said brightly, linking her arm with the girl's. "It's been a long time. Why don't you come to my table so we can catch up?"

Clover's eyes darted from Rupert, who appeared flummoxed and back to Gabriele. "Sure."

Clover grabbed her things and followed Gabriele towards her table at the back of the room. Gabriele thought Clover might just take this opportunity to leave, but surprised her by pulling up an empty chair and sitting beside her. Gabriele noted that Riley had stepped back to the bar. He stared at Rupert with a look of distaste and Gabriele noticed his fists were curling at his side.

Callum, thankfully, returned to his station by the door.

Rupert swiveled his neck and glared at them. Clover kept her gaze focused on the stage. Gabriele shot him a phony, humorless grin.

Riley announced that there would be a thirty minute break before the next set and encouraged the patrons to take the time to order refills. Gabriele caught how Riley's eyes zeroed in on Clover. Clover didn't seem to notice.

Gabriele sat stiffly beside Clover. She'd meant to rescue the girl from her domineering sometimes boyfriend, but that didn't mean she wanted to be her friend. She didn't think they could ever be friends. What would Clover think if she knew? That her long-time boyfriend had run away to Europe without a word, and had met and married a girl, the girl in the chair beside her now, in just twelve months?

Clover leaned in and said, "You didn't have to do that, but thanks."

Gabriele opened her mouth to say "You're welcome," but a firm hand landed on her shoulder before she could get the words out.

Callum whispered in her ear. "We need to talk." Then he returned to the back of the room by the door where he waited with an impatient stare.

Clover threw Gabriele a questioning look.

She debated whether or not she'd respond to the beckoning. A weariness settled on her and she stifled a yawn.

She would rather not walk home alone this late at night, especially considering the eerie experience she had while walking to the pub earlier. She'd appreciate the escort, but made him wait at least five minutes for good measure, just so he wouldn't think she was doing it for him. Then she said goodnight, taking extra time to thank Ciara.

"No problem. You were great," Ciara said. "Maybe we can jam sometime."

"I'd like that."

From her peripheral, Gabriele could see Callum's growing impatience, his stiff shoulders and overly wide eyes. She faced him and mouthed, "I'm coming."

Callum had an actual torch for when the darkness broke up the distance between street lamps. He didn't say anything and Gabriele waited, perplexed.

"You said you wanted to talk."

"I just didn't want you talking to Clover."

"Why?"

"Because you could hurt her."

His statement made Gabriele wonder if Callum had feelings for his brother's old flame.

"I'm not that insensitive," she said. "Besides, meeting Lennon's old girlfriend hasn't exactly been a thrill for me, either."

"I know."

"So, was it you who followed me here?"

Callum stopped. "You were followed?" The dark intensity that filled his eyes frightened her.

"I thought I heard something. Probably just the wind."

It had gotten windier. Gabriele grabbed a handful of hair

that had blown across her face.

"There's a storm brewing from the east," Callum told her. "It's supposed to get nasty overnight."

As if on cue, a gust of wind blasted through the trees, dislodging loose branches that sprayed on the road before them. Callum put a protective arm around Gabriele, rushing her to the path by her cottage. The structure acted as a windbreaker.

"If I leave you here, do you promise to stay put? Otherwise, I'm going to have to put a tracker on you."

Seriously? A tracker? He was joking, right? "Why do you care?"

"Just stay inside until the weather breaks, okay? The tide can get an unbelievably strong storm surge. Don't even go close to the water."

"Okay, fine. I'll stay inside. I won't go swimming." Gabriele broke away and unlocked her door.

Callum waited until she stepped inside. "Good night, Gabriele."

He sounded almost civil. Gabriele caught his eye, noting a flash of emotion. Concern. Interest.

Affection?

"Good night," she returned softly. She closed the door and greeted the solitude. The wind whistled through the windows and the light she'd just switched on flickered.

Suddenly, she really wished she didn't have to sleep alone.

Girls Night

Then . . .

Gabriele tried to ignore Julia's texts and calls, but her friend was persistent and in the end Gabriele said yes to Julia's invitation to join her and a few of their girlfriends for drinks. "Lennon would want you to," Julia said.

That was the thing about Julia. She wasn't afraid to talk to Gabriele about Lennon. Where almost everyone else avoided talking about her deceased husband, at least to her face, Julia had made it clear from the day of the funeral that she was available to talk about Lennon as much as Gabriele wanted. Julia had lost her brother Jonny when she was ten and all she wanted to do after he died was talk about him. When everyone else was sick of the topic, Gabriele had been there.

"It's like people just want me to forget about him," Julia

had complained.

Gabriele had put her arm around Julia's bony shoulders. "They're just afraid the memories will hurt you."

"The memories don't hurt me, Gabi. It's forgetting the memories that hurt."

"Well, here." Gabriele tugged on Julia's dark ponytail. She had long hair back then, and Julia laughed. Jonny always pulled on her ponytail.

Gabriele had been there for Julia, and Julia had promised to return the favor for as long as it took.

Gabriele read Julia's latest text.

Julia Milch
I promised Ulrich I'd have dinner with him tonight, but drinks and desert later at Ontario's at 20:00?

Ontario was a Canadian-themed restaurant in the middle of the *Altstadt* near the famous *Frauenkirche*, about a twenty-five minute walk away. Ulrich was Julia's boyfriend of three months. He was the reason she hadn't seen that much of Julia lately, but Gabriele didn't mind. It was easier to be alone sometimes.

Gabrielle Baumann-Smith
Okay. I'll meet you there.

Julia Milch
Great! I'll invite Britt and Silke.

Gabriele moaned a little. Britt and Silke were her friends, too, but they always acted so strangely around Gabriele now like they were afraid they might break her if they weren't careful enough.

Gabriele brushed her hair and applied makeup for the first time in ages. It felt strange but good, a sign she was digging out of her hole. She dressed simply in jeans, a blouse and a rust-coloured autumn jacket, adding a burgundy cotton scarf before saying good-bye to her parents.

Shoving fists into her pockets, Gabriele walked down *Alaunstrasse* past the park where the headbangers sat on cement benches with large, sleepy dogs lying at their feet, the Asian restaurants, coffee shops, the Euro store, and around the corner past a Subway restaurant to the intersection at *Albertplatz*.

Occasionally, as she made her way down the tree-lined pedestrian lane, she'd pass a couple or a group of people speaking English and her heart would pinch a little. Except for her English language tours at the museum, Gabriele rarely spoke English to anyone anymore.

Before she knew it, she was crossing the old stone Augustus Bridge. Car tires crunched on the cobblestones as they drove across. Streetcars hummed on their tracks. Double-decker tourist busses slowed so the customers could take in the view of the River Elbe and the awe-inspiring baroque architecture of the *Altstadt*.

Julia was already there when Gabriele arrived, with Silke and Britt sitting on the opposite side of the table. Julia waved Gabriele over and she hugged them all quickly in greeting. Julia scooted down on the red vinyl booth seat to make room for her.

Gabriele removed her scarf and smiled. "How is everyone?" She was the one who was making her friends uncomfortable with her sad life. It was up to her to break the ice and ease their minds.

"We're good," Silke said. She tilted her head and looked imploringly into Gabriele's eyes. "How are you? It must be *so* hard."

"I've had better days," Gabriele admitted.

Britt's eyes were wide and fluttering like she was fighting to find something to say, but afraid of saying the wrong thing. She was saved by the arrival of the server.

A round of drinks and dessert brownies were ordered before the awkward pause landed again.

"My brother's back in town." Britt looked at Gabriele and patted her hand. "And he's single."

Gabriele felt her neck flush. She'd had a crush on Axel once upon a time, back in her teens. But somehow she just couldn't go *there* yet. Maybe she'd date again. Someday. But it certainly wasn't something she could think about *today*. "Oh, uh…"

"Gabriele's not ready to date yet," Julia answered for her. "There's plenty of time for that later."

"Of course," Britt stared at the table looking embarrassed like she'd done exactly what she didn't want to do and said the wrong thing.

"It's okay, Britt," Gabriele said, patting her hand back. "I appreciate you thinking that I'm good enough to date your brother."

Britt laughed nervously. "Oh, yeah. You're good enough for him. It's the other way around I'm not sure about. I'm glad you said no."

Their order arrived and Gabriele took a long sip of her wine.

Julia was the first to dig into her brownie bar. "How was your visit with Lennon today?" Silke and Britt stared at her with wide eyes like they couldn't believe she asked that. That she'd said *his* name out loud. Gabriele felt pity for them.

"It was sad, but good. I dreamed about him this morning again."

"Another make-out dream?" Julia said, winking. Britt gasped and Silke choked on her water.

Gabriele couldn't help but grin. "Yes, of course. But this time he said 'good-bye' and told me to 'Live well'."

"Oh, my goodness, Gabi," Julia said. "He's telling you it's time to move on."

Gabriele sighed. "Yeah, but how?"

Julia nudged her shoulder. "Maybe you need to go on a trip. We should plan a holiday together just us girls."

Gabriele noticed how Britt and Silke stiffened. It was an exciting idea if you had a lot of money and weren't traveling with a grieving widow.

"Actually," Gabriele said, "I got some interesting news today."

Julia smirked. "Do tell."

"Lennon had a will. He left me something."

All the girls leaned in, curious. "What?" Julia demanded. "What did he leave you?"

"A cottage on the southern shore of England."

Julia smacked Gabriele in the arm. "No way!"

"It's true."

Julia's jaw hung loose. "He left you beachfront property?"

Gabriele nodded. "That's what the will said."

Julia squealed. "Oh my goodness, Gabi, you've got to go. You're going, aren't you?"

"Lennon said in the will that he wanted me to sell it. It's probably worth a lot. It would be nice to have some money."

"But you're going to go see it first, right? You must be dying to see it." Julia was nearly hyperventilating. "I know I would."

"Yes," Gabriele said. "I'm curious. But what would be the point?"

"The point is you get to spend time in a cottage on the beach in England. You get to leave Dresden for a while, which would do you some good in my opinion. You get a glimpse into Lennon's past, which I know you want. You get *closure*, Gabi." Julia tugged on one of her short dark pigtails and stared hard into Gabriele's eyes. "You *have* to go."

Silke's soft voice broke through Julia's intensity. "Where in England is your cottage?"

"It's in a village called Emsworth."

"Oh," Britta said, "It sounds regal."

"I really don't know anything about it," Gabriele admitted. "I haven't even looked it up online."

"Why not?" Julia asked.

Gabriele shrugged. "I wasn't planning on going."

Julia dug into her purse and removed a smartphone. "I have data," she said. Her thumbs raced across the keyboard. "Here is a satellite map. Wow. It looks quaint. Lot's of water front."

Julia passed her phone around. Gabriele took it last and stared at it for a long time. The town did look quaint. She imagined Lennon playing on the beach there as a child. What was it about this town that Lennon despised so much that he refused to go back? That he didn't even want to speak of the place to her?

"You think I should go?" Gabriele asked softly.

Julia lifted a forkful of brownie. "Most definitely."

LEAVE A LIGHT ON

Callum really didn't want to leave Gabriele alone. Their friendship, if you could call it that, didn't make room for invitations to sleep over in one's spare room. If the wind hadn't turned bitterly cold, he'd consider camping out on her front step.

He sighed and headed through the trees to his house. He flicked on the lights as a warning to any would-be intruders that he was home. He should've told Gabriele to leave a light on. He withdrew his phone from his pocket and texted.

Callum Jones
Leave a light on overnight tonight

A few moments later.

Gabriele Baumann

Why?

Callum studied her name. She'd dropped the Smith. Interesting.

Callum Jones
Just as a precaution.

Gabriele Baumann
A precaution against what?

Damn. Couldn't she just do what he asked her to for once?

Callum Jones
Just a precaution!

Gabriele Baumann
Okay. Fine. Keep your shorts on.

Callum couldn't help the grin that crept onto his face. This girl had spunk. The way she came to Clover Swift's rescue was impressive. Especially since Gabriele knew who Clover was. Most girls would've just watched the drama unfold and not felt a compulsion to help their husband's ex.

He was starting to see why Mick had been so smitten.

Callum removed his jacket but kept his shoes on, rubbing the soles on the mat to clean them. He took a moment to make himself a tuna sandwich that he washed down with a glass of milk. He was tempted to pour himself a drink from his father's whiskey collection. Callum opened the liquor cabinet, twisted a cap off a bottle and sniffed. The smell reminded him of his father. Joe Leatherby enjoyed a nightcap before bed each night. Callum could picture the older man sitting on the deck in the summer, watching the moon reflect over the channel as he sipped the amber liquid and said good night to the day. On cooler evenings, he'd put his feet up on the coffee table in front of the telly and watch Sky News.

A hollow ache folded over in his chest. He missed his father deeply and his brother, too. They didn't always get along, but for the most part, they were close, as close as three guys could get, anyway. They debated and laughed, and didn't hesitate to tease each other, but they had each other's back.

Callum missed Mick's weekly check-ins. He'd followed Mick's love affair from the first day he met Gabriele Baumann while traveling through Germany. Mick's stories about his bungling efforts to learn the language and to fit in with the culture were amusing. Some of his tales were hilarious and made Callum chortle out loud, but underneath there was always the tone of the seriousness of the situation. Mick struggled with homesickness and often felt like a refugee, but he claimed that having Gabriele in his life made it bearable.

Callum had been glad Mick found love again—he had always been the romantic one of their duo—but he had worried it would end badly.

And it had.

Now the woman he blamed for his brother's death was right next door. Try as he might, he couldn't seem to get rid of her. Worse yet, he was starting to fancy her. Even walking close to her that evening had set his nerves alight. When she hugged him yesterday, sobbing into his chest, she almost blew his circuits. He breathed in her shampoo and if she hadn't been the source of his own personal pain, he might've embraced her back. The war in his mind and body was definitely on.

Callum put the whiskey back in the cupboard and made himself a cup of coffee. He didn't drink when he was on assignment. He needed all his senses on alert. And Gabriele was his assignment.

She thought she'd been followed. It might've been her imagination, but Callum worried it was not. He had good reason to believe that Gabriele Baumann's life was in danger. For the sake of his brother's memory, Callum had to keep her safe.

THE CALLAHANS

Ciara waved Gabriele over when she walked into the pub the next morning. "Don't tell me you're drinking beer for breakfast again. That's a bad habit to form."

Gabriele smirked. "No, I'm not here for beer this time. I'd like two eggs on toast."

"You got it." Ciara called the order into the kitchen. Gabriele sat at a table between the bar and the stage and removed her jacket. The storm that had threatened the night before turned out to be a false alarm. The wind continued to be a nuisance, but not hazardous. The sun had disappeared behind a grey and misty gloom she'd associated with England.

Gabriele eyed the guitar on stage and remembered her short performance warmly. Ciara called from behind the bar. "You can play it if you like."

Gabriele glanced around. The bar was on the empty side for a change. It felt strange sitting at the table alone, so she took up Ciara's offer and retrieved the guitar. She was comforted by playing, picking out melodies and humming along. She closed her eyes and for a few minutes she let herself slip away from the craziness her life had become.

Ciara arrived with her breakfast and pulled up a chair beside Gabriele. Gabriele handed her the guitar. "Play for me."

Ciara pierced her with her dark eyes. "You want me to serenade you while you eat?"

"Sure, why not?" Gabriele looked pointedly at the near empty room. "It's not like it's busy."

Ciara grinned, hugged the guitar on her lap and began to play. Gabriele smiled back at her. "You're really good, you know. Do you have ambitions beyond this bar?"

Ciara pursed her lips. "Sometimes. It's a pretty far-fetched dream."

"Tell me."

"I'd like to go to America."

"Really?"

"I know. It's a dumb dream."

"It's not a dumb dream, Ciara. If you want to do it, you should."

"Hey, is this what I'm paying you for?" Riley pulled up a chair and nudged his sister's shoulder. "Leave you alone for a minute and you bunk off."

Ciara ran her fingers along the strings of the guitar before handing it to Riley. He took a turn picking out a riff.

"It's so cool that you both play," Gabriele said as she wiped her mouth with a serviette.

HEART & SOUL

"We come from a musical family," Riley said as his fingers danced along the strings. He had a way of tapping the guitar and making it hum.

"There's six of us kids," Ciara said. "I'm the youngest."

Riley laughed. "Which explains why she's so spoiled."

"Wow, six kids? What was that like growing up?"

"Busy," Ciara said.

Riley added, "Loud."

Ciara nodded. "Chaotic."

Gabriele was intrigued. "Sounds fun. Tell me about your siblings."

"Maeve's the oldest, and my only sister. The rest are all stinky boys." She looked at Riley and laughed.

He smirked. "She means the other brothers. I'm obviously an exception."

Gabriele chuckled. "Obviously."

"Grady's next," Ciara said. "He's a priest."

"A priest in the family? Interesting."

Riley ran a hand through dark hair. "Confession is convenient, especially after a couple o'pints."

"Mikey and Finn are twins, and they're pure trouble."

The way Ciara's eyes shadowed over when she said it made Gabriele believe that she wasn't simply kidding around.

"They're all still in Ireland," Riley added quickly. "We're the only two who've left."

The Riley siblings looked up in tandem when the door chime rang, the signal that another customer had arrived. Gabriele cranked her neck and groaned.

Callum. Again.

Ciara eyed her. "What's up with you two?"

"He's my annoying neighbour."

Ciara cocked a brow. "That was why you asked about the Leatherby boys?"

Gabriele nodded.

"Why did you think their last name was Jones? Or was it Smith?"

"Just a misunderstanding."

Callum walked straight over to their table. His hair was damp from the drizzle and he had bags under his eyes. "Hey," he said, nodding to Ciara and Riley.

"How's it going?" Riley asked before carrying the guitar back to the stage.

"All right."

"You look rough," Gabriele said.

"Yeah, not sleeping enough lately."

Gabriele squinted. Did that have something to do with her?

"Can I get you a coffee?" Ciara offered.

"Please. Two creams, two sugars."

Gabriele leaned back and crossed her arms. "You're persistent, I'll give you that."

Callum grunted.

Ciara sat a steamy, creamy mug of coffee down in front of Callum and asked playfully, "So stranger, are you in town long?"

Callum answered, "It depends."

Gabriele frowned. She knew it depended on her for some reason.

"It's been a while since we've seen you around these parts," Ciara continued.

"My job keeps me in the city."

"What do you do?"

"City of London sustainability."

"Sounds...interesting."

"Very," he said without making eye contact.

"Okay, then," Ciara said when Callum failed to be more forthcoming. "We'll see you guys later." She left a bill and carried away Gabriele's dirty dishes.

"I'm just going to write off your rudeness to you not being a morning person," Gabriele said, "even though it's almost noon."

"I wasn't rude. I just don't think what I do and when I do it is anybody else's business."

"She was just being friendly."

"And I wasn't unfriendly. Just to the point."

"And how's this as to the point: I'm not leaving today."

Callum grunted. "Why am I not surprised?"

"Good." Gabriele felt her phone buzz and removed it from her pocket while saying, "I'm glad we got that sorted."

Julia Milch
Well??

Gabriele Baumann
I'm staying a little longer.

Julia Milch
*Dinner must've went well *wink* At least send me a pic of the brother.*

Callum watched her. "Who are you texting?"

"My friend Julia." Gabriele held up her phone, took a photo of Callum and sent it to Julia.

His brows shot up in alarm. "What are you doing?"

"She wants to see what you look like. Don't tell me you have the same photo phobia as Lennon. Which surprises me, by the way, considering all the photo albums in your house. You guys didn't grow up camera shy."

Julia Milch

You've got to be kidding?????

Gabriele Baumann
Nope. Identical twins.

Julia Milch
WAAAAA

Gabriele Baumann
Believe me, I know.

Callum set his empty mug down with a thud. "What are you telling her?"

"That you are charming and delightful," she said snidely, "the best neighbour *ever*."

Julia Milch
You must be really messed up right now.

Gabriele Baumann
You could say that.

Julia Milch
Is he why you're staying?

Gabriele Baumann
Yes, but not for the reasons you think.

Julia Milch
What other reason is there???

    Callum threw her a look of annoyance before going to the bar to pay for his coffee. Gabriele sighed.

Gabriele Baumann
It's complicated.

Julia Milch
I bet. Oh, boo. Ulrich just got here. I have to go. Call me later!

    Callum returned to their table just as Gabriele put her phone away.

    "Are you ready to go?" he said.

    She scowled at him as she put her jacket on. "Since when are you my babysitter?"

    "Since you refuse to leave the country."

    "About that. Are you ever going to tell me what's going on?"

    "I have a feeling I don't have a choice."

    Ciara walked by with an order belonging to a nearby table. "See you guys around."

    "I still need to pay my bill," Gabriele said.

    Ciara spoke over her shoulder. "It's been paid. Callum covered it."

    Gabriele squinted at Callum. "You didn't have to do that, but thanks."

    He shrugged and held open the door.

A PRETTY BRITISH BOY

Then...

"You freak out every year," Gabriele said to Julia with a knowing smile, "and every year you love it. Come on. It's practically tradition. You have to."

Gabriele pushed Julia to the front of the line despite her protests. Julia twisted the single dark side-braid that hung over her left shoulder. "I don't know why I let you talk me into this every year. You know I'm afraid of heights."

The Ferris wheel stopped in front of them, swinging slightly. Gabriele tugged Julia inside by the hand. "You love it."

"I hate it."

Julia squealed as their bucket lifted higher. Gabriele laughed and ran fingers through her short, bleach-blond hair, feeling free. She raised her arms high above her head and inhaled deeply. The air had a nostalgic smell: a cooling, hot summer day; the sweet scent of cotton candy, roasted nuts and fruity drinks; and the savory aroma of bratwurst sausages and beer. Eighties music was piped into the ride, but above it the fairgrounds along the Elbe River were filled with chatter, laughter and the bells and whistles of a variety of game booths.

Julia gripped the bar in front of her with two hands, knuckles glowing white in the soft moonlight. "If I fall out, my blood is on your hands."

Gabriele patted her on the shoulder. "Don't look down. Look over."

They'd reached the top of the wheel. In front of them was a perfect, unobstructed view of Dresden, *Altstadt*, with its majestic baroque buildings gussied up in lights as if it were a debutante dressed in a gorgeous, expensive gown for her ball. Automobile traffic was halted for the fair and the Augustus Bridge was packed with pedestrians crossing the river that sparkled like a priceless necklace strung between the stone arches.

"You're right, Gabi." Julia breathed out. "It's beautiful. Thank you for making me do this."

Gabriele bought them both a beer at one of the nearby kiosks as a reward and to help Julia calm her nerves. She'd just taken a sip when she felt a body bump into her from behind.

"Excuse me," the male voice said in English. Gabriele turned and replied back in English, "It's fine." Her mouth dropped open slightly when she took in the face of the voice's owner. Handsome features surrounded by shaggy, unkempt dark hair. His eyes, almost black in the dim light, seemed to pierce her and she felt an unfamiliar but not at all unpleasant tremor in her belly.

"You speak English," the guy said with a note of relief. "Maybe you can help me?" He removed a heavy-looking backpack and set it on the ground at his feet before retrieving a mobile phone from his pocket.

"I'm trying to find this hostel." He held out his phone and Gabriele stepped nearer to view it. "My navi doesn't seem to be working and it brought me here." He grinned. "Obviously, not the right place."

Gabriele couldn't help but smile in return. "Yes, I know it," she said. It was not far from where she lived, but she wasn't ready to tell that to a complete stranger—no matter how attractive he was or how endearing his British accent. She gave him directions.

"Thank you," he said, shoving his phone away. "Would it be too forward of me to join you for a beer? I meant to buy one anyway."

Gabriele somehow doubted that he'd gotten lost and accidentally ended up at the city's biggest annual fair of the year, but she couldn't stop the guy from buying a beer. She shrugged and said, "Sure."

"He's cute," Julia said when the guy had left to get in queue.

Gabriele nodded. "He is, isn't he? I wonder what his story is?"

"Why don't you just ask him?"

She didn't have to wait long before the handsome tourist returned.

"My name's Lennon Smith," he said, stretching out a hand.

Gabriele shook his hand. His grip was warm and strong. "I'm Gabriele. This is my friend Julia. She doesn't speak English that well, but she understands quite a bit."

Lennon shook Julia's hand. "Hello." His dark gaze moved back to Gabriele. "Are you from around here?"

"Yes, Dresden is our home."

"Such a beautiful place."

"How about you?"

"England, as you probably gathered from my accent, but I'm planning to remain in continental Europe for some time."

Gabriele's gaze darted to his backpack. "Have you been traveling long?"

"A few months." He took a sip of his beer. "Your English is very good. Did you learn it in school?"

"Everyone takes English in school, and of course, we hear a lot of it in music and in movies, but I'm studying languages in university. I have one more year to go."

"Languages? What else do you speak besides German and English?"

"French, Spanish and Italian."

"That's so cool. I want to learn a second language. I took a little French in school, but now I wish I'd taken German."

His lips tugged up in a way that weakened Gabriele's knees.

Julia was quiet, but Gabriele could tell by the glint in her eyes that she understood everything. Especially what wasn't being said. She felt attracted to this Lennon Smith and she was fairly certain by the signals he was giving off that he felt the same way.

"I think we should *show* him how to get to his hostel," Julia said in German with a mischievous grin.

Lennon's dark eyebrows arched slightly in question, like he knew Julia had said something about him.

Gabriele ignored her friend. She smiled back at Lennon. "Are you traveling alone?"

Lennon nodded and took a quick drink. He didn't expand and Gabriele sensed he didn't want to discuss why he was going solo. It explained why he'd be lonely and wanting to chat with the first person he met who spoke English. Her heart softened a little.

"Julia and I are heading in the direction of your hostel. We could walk with you if you like."

Lennon's smile brightened his face. "I'd love the company." He hoisted his pack over one shoulder, not letting his gaze leave Gabriele's face. "Lead the way."

By the time Gabriele and Julia said good-bye to Lennon that night, Gabriele had agreed to meet him for lunch the next day. Lennon had invited Julia as well, but Julia made up an excuse at the last minute, pretending to have an appointment she'd forgotten, thereby coercing Gabriele to meet him on her own.

Not that she was afraid of him. She just wasn't interested

in getting involved romantically with someone who was clearly passing through town. She met him at the Turkish restaurant and it was the first thing she addressed after they ordered.

"I don't do flings or one-night stands."

Lennon jerked back and studied her with wide eyes. "Good to know. Neither do I."

She cocked her head suspiciously. "Really? Are you saying I'm the first girl you've asked to lunch since you began your solo trek?"

"You are actually."

Gabriele narrowed her eyes. "Why should I believe you?"

"What if I told you I'm thinking of staying in Dresden?"

"Why would you do that? Don't you have a job back in England?"

"Not anymore. I don't want to go back there, either. My plan was to travel Europe until I found the place I wanted to stay. Set up a new home. Dresden is as good a place as any."

"But you don't speak German."

He grinned. "You're a language specialist. I can hire you to teach me."

Gabriele suddenly found it hard to breathe. Was this handsome, British boy planning to stay in Dresden because of her?

Not that she minded. She took a sip of her sparkling water and studied him behind her glass. He leaned back casually in his chair and raked his fingers through his dark, unruly hair. No, she definitely didn't mind. A pretty, British boy was something she would be happy to clear her calendar for.

Lennon grinned crookedly at her with amusement in his eyes as if he could read her mind. She felt a blush burn across her cheeks and took another long sip of water.

A KINK IN THE PLAN

Gabriele fully expected to see Callum's face on the other side of the door when she heard the knocking. She didn't have any friends here other than Ciara, and she was really more of an acquaintance than a friend. Besides, Ciara seemed to live to work and Gabriele had yet to spot her anywhere in Emsworth besides Callahan's Irish Pub. Callum had informed her that the house on the other side was rented out to vacationers and had been quiet and dark since Gabriele arrived. She paused to look in the mirror that hung near the entrance and ran her fingers through her hair. She wished she had time to put on a little lip gloss, but the knocking started up again and she couldn't keep him standing outside too long without him getting suspicious or worried.

Her jaw dropped when she opened the door to Julia's wide smile.

"Surprise!"

"Julia?"

"Yes, it's me!" She squealed and threw herself into Gabriele's friendly embrace.

Gabriele pulled back and stared into Julia's bright eyes. "What are you doing here?"

"Are you going to invite me in?"

"Of course, come in."

Julia sauntered in with just a backpack on her back. "So this is the inheritance," she said, taking in the cozy space. "Nice. And right on the beach! I didn't know you'd be this close."

"Yeah, it's kind of great."

She barged in and took in the place like she owned it. "It's cute. I can see why you're hesitant to sell. Besides the *other* reason."

"The sea air is growing on me." Gabriele worked to control her shock. It was just weird to see her German friend here in her cottage in Emsworth and to be speaking German again. "Can I get you something?"

"Nah, they fed me breakfast on the plane. Show me my room. I need to freshen up and then we need to *talk*."

Gabriele led her to the empty bedroom. "How long are you staying?"

"Just one night. I have to go back to work on Monday. After we talked yesterday, I looked up flights to London on impulse and there was this great, last minute seat sale. I thought to myself, *This is a sign!* The train ride here was pretty straightforward."

"It's great to see you, but you know, you didn't have to interrupt your plans to check up on me. I'm okay. Really."

"Gabriele, you've had a big shock. I'm your friend. Of

course, I would come. And it wasn't a big inconvenience at all. I'm excited to get away for a little while."

"Okay, well now that you're here, what do you want to do?"

Julia flashed a mischievous smile. "I want to meet your neighbour naturally."

Gabriele swallowed. She wasn't ready to make that particular introduction. Julia would judge, come to conclusions, say something about Lennon—she wasn't always the most tactful person.

"He works during the day."

"Even on weekends?" Julia questioned.

"I'm picking up that he's a bit of a work-a-holic."

"So, you don't see him that much?"

Actually, at first she saw him more than she wanted. Now, she felt like she wouldn't mind a little more of his attention. But she didn't want Julia to know that, and they'd been friends for so long, it was hard to hide anything from her. She had a freaky way of reading her mind sometimes. "It's a small town. I'm sure we'll run into him eventually."

"Then show me around the town!"

The weather had calmed enough that Gabriele thought it'd be safe to take a turn on the promenade. Julia had the foresight to pack an umbrella and Gabriele grabbed a spare one she'd found in one of the cupboards.

She showed Julia the steps that led down to the beach. Julia stared back at the cottage from the damp shoreline. "Which one is his?"

Gabriele didn't have to ask to whom she was referring. She pointed to the house next door with the terrace light left on. "That one."

"A close neighbour."

Gabriele nodded. "Too close." She grabbed her friend's arm and they padded over the broken shells and shiny wet pebbles.

"I love this smell," Julia said. Then she pointed to two rows of short, old boards visible with the tide out so far.

"Those are old oyster beds. Apparently it used to be a big industry in the 1800s."

Julia wrinkled her nose. "I'm not a fan of oysters."

"I think they are an acquired taste."

They made it to the promenade and began the walk that divided the sea from the manmade pond. They were passed by a couple joggers and a mother pushing a stroller. Some of the sailboats on the seaside lay like the elderly in need of hip replacements. Others were tied to buoys farther out and had enough water to maintain their dignity and remain upright. The misty fog that billowed between added an eerie element.

"It's beautiful," Julia said. "I can imagine how gorgeous it must be in good weather."

"It was sunny when I first arrived and it was lovely," Gabriele admitted.

"So that's your cottage and Lennon's identical twin brother lives next door." Julia eyed Gabriele carefully. "What's your next move?"

"Honestly, I'm torn. Part of me wants to keep it because it's cool to have something right on the sea." She chuckled. "Under different circumstances, I might even be able to relax."

"How often do you think you would come?"

Gabriele shrugged. "That's the thing. Not enough to merit keeping it. There are a number of nice places to stay if I really want to come back. It's not necessary to own."

"But…"

"But nothing. I just want answers first."

"To what questions?"

Gabriele bit the inside of her lip. "For one, why didn't Lennon tell me he had a brother? And secondly, why didn't he want me to know about this place? Why didn't he tell me about his girlfriend?"

"That's three questions. Who's the girlfriend?"

Gabriele shot her a look.

Julia corrected, "I mean former girlfriend."

"Her name's Clover Swift."

"And…"

"And nothing." Gabriele didn't want to point out the hair similarities or her fear that she'd been Clover's replacement.

"I totally understand your need to know. And the brother Callum? He can't answer?"

Gabriele's gaze cut to the Leatherby house. She wouldn't be surprised if Callum were spying on her with his binoculars.

"So far his lips have been sealed, but I'm working on him. That's why I need to stay. I think he's starting to warm up to me."

Julia rubbed her arms. "Speaking of warming up, I'm freezing. And hungry. Is there a place we can eat?"

They turned around and headed into town. Gabriele led Julia to Callahans and they found a booth near the bar. Ciara was tending again and Gabriele waved. "Hi Ciara."

"Hi Gabriele."

"This is my friend Julia from Dresden."

"Welcome to Emsworth," Ciara said with a smile.

"She seems nice," Julia said quietly when Ciara had turned.

"She is."

Julia grinned crookedly. "My British counterpart?"

Gabriele rolled her eyes.

One of the servers approached and Gabriele ordered fish and chips for both of them. Julia gaped.

"You can't come to England and not eat fish and chips," Gabriele explained.

They took turns using the loo where they touched up their makeup. They were thoroughly warmed up and had raging appetites by the time their food arrived.

"So when do I get to meet this mystery brother?" Julia asked as she tossed a fry into her mouth.

Gabriele nodded with her chin. "He's right over there behind you."

Julia swiveled around and stared. Callum lifted his fingers in a weak wave as acknowledgement. Julia spun back around.

"Oh my God, Gabi. He looks just like Lennon! How can you stand it?"

"I've spent enough time with him now that I know he's not

HEART&SOUL

Lennon. He's not just different in personality, but also in looks if you check closely. After a while, the differences become so pronounced, you stop seeing Lennon and just see Callum."

Julia stared hard at her friend. "You've thought this through."

"It's true."

"When did he arrive?"

"About twenty minutes ago."

"And you didn't say anything?"

Gabriele shrugged a shoulder. "I'm getting used to him hovering. I told you he'd show up."

"The guy's a stalker?" Julia twisted one of her short, dark pigtails. "That's creepy, Gabi. Maybe Lennon and Callum are like Dr. Jekyl and Mr. Hyde. Maybe where Lennon was all goodness, Callum is the evil twin."

Gabriele laughed, but it wasn't like the same thought hadn't occurred to her. However, Callum had plenty of chances to act on any evil impulses he may have had and he seemed to be sincerely concerned for her well-being. Even if that concern was misplaced.

It was like he knew they were talking about him. He stood, shoved fists into his pockets and sauntered over. Julia gasped audibly when Callum slid in beside Gabriele.

"This is too weird," Julia spouted in rapid German. "I don't see the difference. I feel like I'm seeing a ghost!"

Callum's brow furrowed. "What's she saying?"

"He doesn't understand what you're saying," Gabriele said to Julia in German, "thankfully."

"Good. Then I can tell you that he's super hot. Lightning strikes twice for you."

"Well, I'm not interested."

"Oh." She batted her eyes at Callum. "Too bad I'm taken."

"As fun as this is," Callum said, "any chance of switching to English?" He nudged Gabriele's leg with his knee. "How about introducing me to your friend?"

Gabriele's face grew warm. It was just a leg tap, but it felt incredibly friendly, shooting sparks through her body. His closeness was like radiation. Why was she reacting like this? She swallowed hard and forced her expression to remain blank. "This is my friend Julia," she said in English. "She doesn't speak English very well, but she understands a lot. Julia, this is Callum."

"Nice to meet you," Callum said.

Julia extended a hand and said in heavily accented English, "Nice to meet you, too."

"You're here to visit for how long?"

Gabriele noted the concern in Callum's eyes. A lengthy visit would put a kink into his plan to extract her.

Gabriele answered for her. "She came to check up on me for one day, that's how good a friend she is. She has to leave tomorrow."

Callum's jaw relaxed, apparently happy with the answer. "I hope you enjoy your visit to Emsworth."

He leaned back and casually let his arm rest along the back of the booth behind Gabriele's back. He motioned to a server to bring him a beer and didn't see Julia's eyes widen in question, though Gabriele thought he had to be aware of her body stiffening at his friendly gesture.

"Are you sure there's nothing going on between you?" Julia asked in German.

Gabriele shook her head. "I'd tell you if there were."

"If I had to go on the way he's looking at you *right now*," Julia said pointedly, "I'd say I don't believe you."

Gabriele's eyes cut back to Callum. He was looking at her with something of a glint in his eye. His lips turned up slightly. "Do you want anything else? Your lunch and Julia's are on me."

Gabriele's jaw dropped. She hadn't seen this version of Callum before. This friendly, easygoing version. She narrowed her eyes. "What are you up to?"

"What? Can't a guy buy a couple pretty girls their lunch?"

"What happened to the mean Callum intent on scaring the new girl out of town?"

His grin grew wider. "Turns out the new girl is tougher than he thought."

ABOVE THE WIND AND RAIN

Julia turned up her nose at Gabriele. "These are the best buns you could find?"

"They don't have a German bakery here, or, if they do, I haven't had a chance to discover it." Gabriele spread butter on her bun and added a slice of meat. "Can you pass me the juice?"

She pressed her palm against her mouth as she yawned. She and Julia had stayed up way too late talking last night. She had to throw her pillow at her friend more than once. Julia was such a crazy romantic. She had Gabriele alternately married to Callum Leatherby and running for dear life before midnight.

Gabriele had clicked on the television to catch the morning news and it hummed in the background of their subdued conversation: the young royal family at a petting zoo on a visit to Australia, the Prime Minister of Israel in London to meet with the British PM, another weather system moving in from the northeast.

HEART & SOUL

"You don't have to walk me," Julia said as she prepared to leave. "I found my way here from the station by myself."

Gabriele wrapped a scarf around her neck. "I don't mind. You've come all this way to see me for one day. It's the least I can do."

It took about twenty minutes. Julia's suitcase made clopping noises as she pulled it along the bumpy pavement, past the Irish pub, through the center of town and into the pedestrian underpass that circumvented the busy cross street.

They paused to admire the Emsworth quay murals that took up the surface area of both walls. "This looks like your cottage," Julia said and they slowed their pace.

Gabriele squinted. "It might be."

Julia stood at the ticket window to purchase her ticket on the national railway to the London City Airport.

"Let me get that," Gabriele said as she pulled out her wallet.

Julia slapped her hand away. "You don't have to do that."

"It's the least I can do."

"I came uninvited," Julia said.

"I loved that you came."

"I'm the one with the job."

Gabriele couldn't argue that one.

"I'll buy you and Ulrich dinner when I get home."

Julia smiled. "I'm glad to hear you're coming back. Does that mean you're selling?"

"Eventually. There are still some things I want to find out."

"From your closed-lipped neighbour?"

Gabriele nodded, but she had to work at not thinking about her neighbor's actual lips. She shook her head sharply. What was the matter with her?

Julia bought her ticket and Gabriele waited with her on the platform. The wind had picked up again quite suddenly and the sky overhead darkened noticeably. "You may be getting out of England just in time," Gabriele said.

Julia nodded. "Looks like you might be in for a storm."

Gabriele exhaled. She had a feeling that the same statement could be true metaphorically, as well.

Julia looked at Gabriele kindly. "Be careful with your heart, my friend."

"I'm not going to fall for him, Julia. You don't have to worry."

"Maybe you should."

"You think I should date Lennon's brother? What about being careful with my heart?"

"It can go both ways. Maybe dating him would be a bad idea. But maybe not dating him is equally bad, if you won't do it just because… you know."

"You're the queen of giving conflicting advice today."

"Just don't rush into anything. Either way."

Gabriele smiled and squeezed her friend. "Your train is coming. Have a good trip home."

It started to rain as Gabriele walked back to the cottage. She sprung open the umbrella she had tucked into her purse. The *tap, tap* on the nylon surface was soothing. Her mind returned to Julia's confusing piece of advice. *Be careful not to fall for Callum just because he's Lennon's brother and looks like Lennon. Be careful not to stop yourself from falling for Callum just because he's Lennon's brother and looks like Lennon.*

How on earth was she to navigate that kind of land mine?

Her mind was so captivated by this train of thought that

she almost missed seeing the very object of her consternation leaning against the rail at the opening of the underground walkway. Her eyes fluttered along with her heart when she registered it was Callum resting there with arms crossed against his blue jacket.

Gabriele gave him a look. "I'm beginning to think I need to get a restraining order." She didn't slow as she walked past him. He fell into stride beside her.

"Just making sure you make it back okay."

"Why wouldn't I make it home okay?"

He lowered his voice as he entered the underpass. "You thought you were being followed before."

"It was just a cat or something," Gabriele said, but her mind flashed to another time, with Lennon. They were walking home after dark, just a week or so before Lennon died, and she noticed how he kept looking over his shoulder. He did it in such a way as to not be obvious about it, but she remembered thinking he was acting oddly. He had his hand on her lower back and pushed her to speed up her pace. She'd chalked it up to stress from work and his growing trouble with insomnia, but now...

They exited the underpass and Gabriele's hair whipped across her face. She held the umbrella higher and motioned for Callum to join her underneath.

He ducked in, relieving Gabriele of the task of holding the umbrella, wrapping his arm around her shoulder to do so.

He spoke into her ear, "This storm could be bad."

His closeness was unnerving, but she appreciated his willingness to shield her from the weather. She shoved cold hands into her pockets and stayed close to Callum's side.

They were both cold and wet by the time they reached her

front door.

Gabriele deliberated with herself as he hovered beside her. Should she invite him inside? He had insinuated that he might tell her the truth and now would be a great time, in her book. She just wished it were nice enough to sit outside. Being alone together felt too… friendly.

She imagined he felt as awkward as she did. But they were adults. They could deal.

She tilted her head and caught his eye. "Would you like to come inside?"

Callum simply nodded.

Gabriele hung her jacket in the closet, replacing it with a warmer, drier cardigan. Callum draped his coat over the back of a kitchen chair. Yes. The kitchen was less intimate than the living room.

"Can I get you a coffee?" Gabriele offered. "I'm making myself one."

"Sure."

Gabriele put the hot water kettle on the stove and scooped grounds into the Bodem carafe. She leaned against the counter and crossed her arms, watching Callum as he sat stiffly at the table. His eyes flickered to hers and they locked gazes. His expression was cool and intense. His likeness to Lennon made her heart leap, but she didn't mistake Callum for his brother. The man before her was practically a stranger.

An attractive, alluring, enigmatic stranger.

He glanced away to retrieve his phone from his pocket, glancing at the name of the caller.

"Excuse me," he said, standing. "I have to take this."

He disappeared into the living room, but his low tenor voice echoed across the high beams of the slanted ceiling and

Gabriele could make out a few words.

"... when did this happen?... whereabouts of Sati Habib... I have to deal with the girl..."

The girl? Gabriele stiffened. Was she the girl?

Her stomach tightened. She hated feeling like she was being managed. The whistle blew, startling her and she poured the hot water over the grounds.

Gabriele flashed Callum an angry glare when he returned to the table.

"Is something wrong?" he asked.

"Am I *the girl?*"

Callum's shoulders jerked and his jaw twitched. "You weren't supposed to hear that," he said.

"Well, I did. And I want answers, Callum. You are driving me crazy!"

Callum ran a hand over his head and held his neck. "Why are you so stubborn?"

She shot back, "Why are you so secretive?"

"I'm just trying to protect you."

"Maybe I want to protect myself. It would help a lot if I knew what I was protecting myself from."

"The less you know, the safer you'll be. Just trust me for once, Gabriele." He grabbed his coat. "It's in your best interest to leave England as soon as possible." He softened his tone. "I'm not leaving Emsworth until you do, so, let me know when you're ready to go and I'll drive you to the airport."

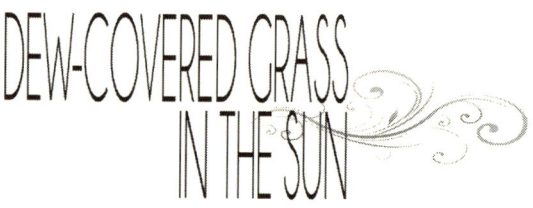

DEW-COVERED GRASS IN THE SUN

Gabriele startled awake to banging on the door. At first she thought it was the storm that had gathered steam overnight. The wind whistled through the bedroom window and the nearby bush scratched aggressively against it. The banging persisted and Gabriele fussed with a cardigan overtop of her pajamas as she rushed for the door yelling, "Who is it?"

"Callum!"

Of course it was him, but she'd wanted to make sure. He'd put the fear of the boogey man in her.

She unlatched the locks and Callum blew in with a good amount of sand.

"The storm is worse than was originally forecasted. You need to come with me to my house."

"Why?"

"It's set back further inland and has two floors. There's a danger the tidal surge could flood the cottage."

"Really? It's happened before?"

"Not often, but yes. It's why we buy expensive insurance." He waved a hand. "Hurry. Grab your things."

Outside the patio furniture tumbled loudly along the terrace, setting Gabriele off on high speed to do what Callum requested. She scooped her makeup and toiletries into her overnight bag. She strapped her purse over her shoulder.

"I'm ready."

Callum snapped his umbrella open and pulled Gabriele under his arm. They pushed against the wind and rain through the patch of trees and up the walk to Callum's house, but even with the protection, rain blew at sharp angles and stung her face.

They were both drenched when Callum locked the door against the storm.

Compared to the screeching howl outside, the sudden muffled quiet in Callum's house felt jarring. She watched Callum as he looked at her, his eyes narrow and inquisitive as if he was searching her soul. Water collected like crystal drops on his dark long lashes. It ran in thin rivulets down his temples and along his cheeks. His jaw, so much like Lennon's, was covered in bristles that glistened in the foyer lights like dew-covered grass in the sun. Gabriele stared, mesmerized. He was beautiful.

"Are you okay?"

She snapped to attention, chiding herself. "Yeah, I'm fine. Just wet."

"You know where the loo is if you want to freshen up. There are clean towels in the cupboard."

She remembered where the loo was, though this was her first opportunity to enter it. This time she'd refrain from snooping. At least for now.

The bathroom had a large tub, the old kind with claw feet. It took up most of the space, leaving just enough room for a sink with cupboards underneath and a toilet.

Gabriele had never been more thankful that she'd taken the time to grab her makeup and toiletries bag than she was right now, looking into the mirror. What a horror! No wonder Callum stared at her like that and encouraged her to clean up. She could try out for a role in a zombie film.

She got to work washing her face and brushing out her hair. She applied just a touch of makeup, enough to make her green eyes brighten. She brushed her teeth and felt marginally better. At least she was presentable now.

When she returned to the living room, Callum was crouched down beside the fireplace, stoking a fire. She bent down beside him. "This is nice."

Her coat had taken the worst of the wet weather, but her pajama pants were damp and she shivered. Perhaps she should've grabbed a pair of jeans. Callum stood and returned wearing dry clothes and carrying a blanket. He wrapped it over Gabriele's shoulders, then pushed the sofa closer to the wood stove so they wouldn't have to sit on the floor.

"I'll make coffee."

Gabriele curled up on the sofa, tucking her feet underneath her, and stared at the flames. They danced and crackled and hissed in a way that felt hypnotic. Her mind swirled with emotion as she let herself get drawn in.

Lennon.

Callum.

She'd come to England for closure. Was she finding it?

Callum returned with two steaming mugs in hand and gave her the one with the foam on top.

"You don't have to go to the trouble of foaming the milk," she said softly. "I can drink it the regular way."

"I don't mind. It's not like I have a lot of other business I can do at the moment."

"Your city job seems to be pretty flexible," Gabriele said after her first sip. Callum had barely let her out of his sight since she arrived. "Didn't you say you worked in London?"

Callum twisted from his spot on the other end of the sofa to face her. "I can work from anywhere as long as I have a laptop and internet."

"I see. I was under the impression you didn't like to hang out at this house much?"

He nodded. "That's true. Too many memories."

"Not all bad, I hope."

"No, most of them are good." He sighed. "Those are actually the hard ones."

Gabriele tucked in tighter. "I understand that. My memories of Lennon are good, but they hurt like hell."

Callum leaned forward, resting an elbow on one knee. "Tell me about him. The last year. Tell me what his life was like."

Gabriele eyed him. "I thought you kept in touch?"

"We did, but I'd like to hear it from your perspective."

Gabriele sipped her coffee and closed her eyes, remembering. "He was happy. At least he seemed to be to me. Always smiling. Quiet, didn't talk much. Now that I think about it, I did most of the talking. We spent all our free time together, but I really didn't have that much free time. My workload at uni was heavy and my parents insisted that we spend some of that time with the family. When Lennon and I decided to get married, life got really busy with the wedding plans."

Her mind flashed to an image of Lennon slouching on the sofa with eyes closed and earbuds in his ears. "Though he wasn't a musician, he loved music. Especially the Beatles."

Callum nodded. "That's why he chose the name Lennon."

Right. She kept forgetting his name was really Mick. Could she ever get used to that?

The wind whirled and whistled through worn window panes. The lights from the dated chandelier flickered. Callum left the room and returned shortly with a stubby white candle in a brass stand. "The electricity won't last in a storm like this."

He lit the candle, then laid it and the lighter down on the coffee table.

"Are you going to tell me why he changed his name?" she asked.

He took his place on the sofa and said, "When Mick and I were fifteen our dad took us on holiday to Europe."

Right. He'd mentioned a trip. Not the answer to her question, but she let it go, wanting to hear the story.

"Dad wanted us to be cultured," Callum continued. "Nothing off the beaten path, just the regular tourist stops—Paris, Barcelona and Berlin. I thought it was interesting, but I'd just as soon have stayed at home and partied with my friends. But Mick was enthralled by the history, the architecture and the different languages." Callum laughed. "And the food."

Gabriele considered him. "Was that why he chose to move to Europe?"

"Yes."

Her instincts told her there was more to this story. Much more. She leaned forward and begged, "Please, Callum, tell me what happened. I have to know. Why did he relocate to Dresden? Why did someone kill him?"

Callum's eyes locked on hers and he took in a long, hard breath. "You're not going to give up, are you?"

"No."

He sighed again with resignation. "Mick was in his third year of computer science studies at the University of London. He had a roommate for all those years. Sati Habib."

This was the name she'd heard Callum mention on the phone the day before.

"They became good friends. Chummed around, drank beer after class in the neighbouring pubs. At least that's what they did the first year. The second year Sati became more withdrawn and serious. Mick thought it was just the pressure of his studies. He didn't just want to be in the top of his classes. He wanted to be the best.

"During the summer break after the second year, Sati returned to Syria to visit family. That's what he told Mick he was doing anyway."

Callum rubbed his forehead then glanced up at Gabriele with an intense, conflicted gaze. She knew this was the crux. The information that came next was going to turn her life upside down. She gripped her coffee mug nervously.

"Sati trained with an extreme Islamic group that had formed as a result of the Arab Spring. His mandate on his return was to join an Al Qaeda cell with other British nationals who were sympathetic to their cause and assist in planning a terrorist attack."

Gabriele blinked hard. "What did Lennon have to do with all this?"

"He discovered the plan. Sati had saved the details of the attack on a flash stick, which he left in his desk drawer, hidden in plain sight as they say.

"Except that Lennon had misplaced his and needed one to save a report. He didn't think Sati would mind if he borrowed one from him, so he searched Sati's desk and took the first one he found."

He paused to sip his coffee.

"There were a lot of files on the stick with course names and projects that Mick recognized, but there was one with the title, "London Bridge is Coming Down."

"Mick, always the curious one, clicked on it. That's how he stumbled across their plans to bomb the Tower Bridge."

Gabriele let out a breath. *Meine Güte*. "What did he do?"

"He told me. I'll never forget his frantic voice when he rang me on my mobile. At first he thought Sati was just messing about, but as he read the details of the planned attack and Sati's part in it, he knew it was real. I insisted he approach the police with it at once.

"And that was the beginning of the end. Mick submitted the flash stick to the police department and Sati was arrested and put in prison. A short time later Mick began receiving threatening emails."

"He thought he could hide from a terrorist group in Germany?"

"He didn't just go on a whim, Gabriele. Mick was put in the witness protection program."

Gabriele's mind folded over with slow comprehension. Lennon's name change, the lies about his family, his refusal to visit England. This espionage story was something straight from a movie. She pinched her eyes tight, commanding all the emotions that ran rampant to line up and submit to her control. Lennon was a victim. Wrong place, wrong time. His life was turned upside down. And not only his.

"That's why he left Clover so suddenly without a word?" And the reason he hadn't stayed in Emsworth and married her?

"Yes," Callum said. "The authorities asked Mick where he wanted to go and he said Germany. He started off in Berlin, and took some time to travel around as Lennon Smith." His jaw twitched and his eyes darkened. "Then he met you."

"Does that make you angry?" Gabriele felt all the muscles in her body tighten. She folded her arms across her chest. "I made him happy."

"You made him vulnerable."

"Are you blaming me?"

"Do I believe that if he hadn't married you, had all those silly pictures of himself taken, that he'd still be alive? Did I wish he'd just shagged you and moved on? Yes."

Blood rushed to Gabriele's head and she let out a strangled gasp. That was why Lennon had pushed for a quiet wedding. It was why all the pictures of his face were missing. He'd removed them, trying to cover his trail.

Her eyes welled with tears as her grief turned to remorse. She closed her eyes and curled inwardly into a tight ball. Oh, God. Lennon was dead because of her. Because they had fallen in love. Her chest shuddered as hot tears streamed down her cheeks

"I blamed you because I wanted someone to blame." Callum's voice softened. "The fact is the blame belongs on Sati and the terrorists. It's not your fault."

Callum shifted closer. He took her empty coffee mug and

set it on the table. "Mick couldn't help falling for you. I think I understand that now." His eyes took her in with such intensity, Gabriele's breath hitched. He stroked her hair pushing it off her face and behind her ears, and the touch of his fingertips along her jaw burned a line across her skin. Her throat grew dry and she could barely swallow.

He leaned closer and her heart thundered like a train out of control. If he tried to kiss her, she'd let him. Even though she knew it would be the dumbest thing in the world to do, it was something she suddenly wanted. Her skin ached for his touch. She stared at his lips and tilted her head towards him.

The wind roared, slapping against the house and exploding through the weakened glass of the dining room window with a deafening crash. Glass shattered on the floor. A siren blared. Gabriele screamed.

The lights went out.

YOU LOOK A LITTLE UNCOMFORTABLE

Callum swooped up the candle, dashed to a panel near the front door and quickly tapped in numbers that turned off the alarm.

He returned for Gabriele and took her hand, leading her up the steps and down the hall to the bathroom. "This is the only room without windows. They might all burst out before this storm is through. They're originals and should've been replaced long ago." He put the candle down and eyed Gabriele as he removed his phone from his pocket. He flicked on the torch.

"Wait here. I'll be right back."

Callum dashed to the storage room near the end of the hall and opened the door. He flashed the beam of light coming from his phone onto the contents inside. He gathered a foam camping pad, a large pillow and a blanket, and deftly carried the pile blindly as it filled the area in front of his face. He had no choice but to slip the phone back into his pocket and follow the wall back to the bathroom where Gabriele waited.

Gabriele. He wanted to kiss her. He almost did. Maybe it was a good thing nature intervened. He wasn't sure. He wasn't sure about anything any more. His feelings were betraying him. In two days he moved from being indifferent to regarding Gabriele Baumann, seeing her only as an annoyance that needed to be removed, to struggling with feelings inappropriately directed towards his brother's widow.

All he wanted to do now was to protect her. She projected a tough exterior, but on occasion, like tonight, he spotted her vulnerability. He wanted to keep her safe, ease the pain in her heart and soul.

He wanted her.

He dropped his cargo on the bathroom floor when he entered the bathroom. Gabriele sat on the lid of the toilet, legs and arms crossed. The wind rattled the whole house and she stiffened. She blinked like she was trying to reboot her circuits and her wide-eyed expression flattened. Callum admired the way she tackled fear head on.

"What's that?" she asked.

Callum plucked the camping foam from the pile and laid it on the bottom of the tub. He covered it with a blanket and propped the pillow at the end opposite the faucet.

Then he crawled in.

He sat with his back leaning against the pillow, his long legs bent, his feet propped against the edge of the tub. He grinned at Gabriele as he put his hands behind his head. "Not bad."

She smirked. "Yeah, for you."

"You're right. You do look a little uncomfortable sitting there." His grin deepened. He couldn't stop staring at her. The candlelight reflected the gold flecks in her big green eyes and she stared back like she was mesmerized. His focus locked on her lips and when she self-consciously nibbled on them, heat flushed his body.

"Well, if you were being a good host," she said huskily, "you'd give your guest the best spot in the room."

"Hmm. You're right." He closed his eyes and worked to settle himself down. "I guess I'm not a very good host."

Gabriele threw a towel at him. It landed on his face, but he didn't move. It felt cool and calmed his breathing.

"Oh, *meine Güte*," Gabriele finally said. "You're going to suffocate under that thing."

"If you're worried for my life," he mumbled from beneath it, "perhaps you should remove it."

He heard Gabriele huff. He sensed her movement as she approached. She sat on the edge of the tub and reached for the towel. Callum's arm snapped up and grabbed her wrist. She squealed as he pulled her on top of him.

She let out an adorable giggle. "What are you doing?"

"There's room in here for two. No sense in you being uncomfortable."

He shifted over and her slender form slid in beside him. He left his arm opened, inviting her to nestle in. She looked down at him for the briefest moment before accepting his silent invitation. She nuzzled in and rested her head on his shoulder.

He felt the softness of her body against his and his head rushed with blood. He wasn't certain where to place his hand. With the length of his arm, it naturally landed near the curviest part of her body. He crooked his elbow and laid his arm over her waist, which was a pleasant alternative. His chin rested in her hair and he breathed in the fruity scent of her shampoo. Her palm lay on his chest and his heart beat wildly at her nearness. He knew there was no way he could conceal how she affected him.

"Are you all right?" he choked out.

"Yeah," she whispered. "I'm good."

They lay quietly together in the dim light of the flickering candle, neither of them moving. Gabriele's breath matched his. Callum ran his thumb along the flesh of her arm, relishing her softness, wishing for the first time that things were different. That he had met this girl under different circumstances. That he didn't have to drop her off at the airport the next day and say good-bye forever.

Her fingers drew small circles on his chest and he held in a moan.

Then she broke the silence.

"Why aren't you in witness protection?"

Callum let out a long breath. He didn't actually want to talk about this, but it was a good distraction to where his mind was going. He really needed the distraction.

"I wasn't the one involved directly."

"But you're his brother and you look, or at least you looked, just like him."

"I presented that same argument. Plus, they murdered our father."

Her head popped up and she gawked at him. "He didn't die of a heart attack?"

"No. They injected him with something, just ran into him with a needle as he was walking down High Street, here in Emsworth. He collapsed on the pavement and died before help arrived."

She rested her head against his chest once again. "I'm so sorry."

"Unless I was Lennon's spouse or his child," Callum continued, "they couldn't help me. At least not like that."

"How could they help you?"

"They suggested I join the army."

"Wasn't that as dangerous?"

He chuckled, but not because he thought it was funny. "At least there I was armed. The training was good, made me stronger and faster."

"And you changed your last name?"

"I wanted something too common to be tracked easily. Callum Leatherby no longer exists. I was Corporal Private Callum Jones for almost a year before the troops were pulled out."

She tilted her head to look at him and he was taken in once again by her spectacular eyes.

"Do you really work for the city?" she asked.

Callum shifted and pulled her on top of him. He spoke into her ear. "You know what? You do talk too much."

DRINK, DRINK, DRINK

His lips were on hers before Gabriele knew what was happening. They were warm, soft and tasted of coffee. They belonged to Lennon's brother.

She froze. Her heart rattled. She was legally and morally free to kiss another man, but was she ready? Did she want to kiss *this* man?

Callum pulled back. "I'm sorry."

Gabriele stared at his burning dark eyes. She was an alcoholic hanging onto a bottle of vodka, mesmerized and paralyzed. She should run as far and fast as she could away from the temptation, but God, she wanted a drink.

She traced his eyebrows with her fingers, the bridge of his nose, his cheekbones and the rough surface of his jaw. He had Lennon's face. *He had Lennon's face!*

HEART&SOUL

She wasn't strong enough. She grabbed the shot glass and drank. Her mouth was on his and suddenly she was desperate. She couldn't stop at one glass, she needed the whole bottle.

Callum responded to her urgency. He was thirsty, too. They were both so parched from their pain. The loss of a brother. The loss of a spouse.

She kissed him as if her kisses were keeping them alive. As if, should they stop for one moment, they would have to deal with the truth, with their reality, and with all the horrible agony of the last year. She couldn't bear it.

Callum's lips moved along her jaw and down her neck. She arched her back in response, leaning into him. Her elbows pinched uncomfortably along the porcelain, her knees pressed awkwardly along the curve of the tub. They were like crazed teenagers in the cramped space of a car's backseat.

She kissed him because he *looked* like Lennon. And because he *wasn't* Lennon. And because she was angry *with* Lennon.

Their breath came in fast, hard bursts. She was taking it out on Callum, using him to exorcize her demons. By the way he poured himself into her, she suspected he was using her as well.

She felt her face grow wet with tears. Her heart was breaking all over again and all she could do was drink, drink, drink. She kissed his face, his eyes, his jaw, his lips. Her hands slipped under his shirt, and her fingers spread wide across the firm muscles of his chest. Callum pulled his T-shirt over his head with expertise and tossed it onto the bathroom floor. His eyes narrowed as he took in her face.

"You're crying."

"I know. I'm sorry." She stared back at him. His eyes were glassy with desire, but they flickered with a darkness she didn't want to examine. She bent low and kissed his forehead. His hands rested on the bare skin of her hips. His lips moved along her cheek, wiping up her tears.

She trembled with nerves and passion and a longing that sprung from deep within. She needed to be kissed and touched and wanted. She was a desert after a year of no water. Callum was her thunderstorm. Her moan morphed into an unattractive sob. Loud hiccups echoed in the small room. She tried to control it, knowing how it must appear to Callum.

Her mind split in two: she was somehow both in the situation and watching the situation. She judged herself harshly. She was weak and pathetic. She pressed a palm to her face.

Callum wrapped his arms around her, holding her trembling body tight. She sobbed into his neck. He stroked her hair and let out a long, steady breath. "It's okay, Gabriele."

She willed her heart to slow and her mind to clear. She felt so stupid. Why couldn't she keep her crap together?

She squeezed her eyes shut, stopping the stream of tears that pooled on Callum's shoulder. She felt the pulse in his neck thump against her ear and she could tell he was working to gain control.

"I'm sorry," she said.

"I'm not."

"I wasn't, you know..."

"You weren't what?"

"I was kissing *you*."

It was half true. At moments she had been kissing Lennon, and she grieved his passing. But mostly she had been kissing Callum, and she mourned what she could never have with him. She was a mess and a wreck. She rested her face on his chest.

His lips touched her forehead. "I'm glad."

The candle flickered weakly, reaching the end of its quick. Soon they would be cast into total darkness.

"Do you hear that?" Callum said softly.

All she could hear was the slowing rhythm of his heart. "Hear what?"

"The storm. I think the worst has passed."

Gabriele cocked her head to listen. The storm had abated with quiet slipping in to take its place.

Gabriele gingerly lifted herself off Callum and climbed out of the tub. She stretched the kinks out of her back and ran her fingers through her hair, unsure what she was to do next. She avoided looking in the mirror, not wanting to see the reckless, half-crazed, blurry-eyed woman standing there.

Callum jumped out after her and reached for his T-shirt. He pushed his head through the neck hole, pulling the hem down over his chiseled chest. He raked his hair back with his hands. He faced her and they eyed each other awkwardly.

"I'm not sorry," Callum repeated.

Gabriele didn't know what to say. She *was* sorry. Not because he wasn't Lennon, but because she knew she and Callum never had a chance.

He reached for her hand, wove his fingers through hers. "I wish there was a way..." He paused and the words left unsaid confirmed Gabriele's fears. They would part soon and all this would be over. A memory. Another sweet, bitter memory to add to her collection.

"Me, too."

A deafening siren erupted in the house. Callum stiffened.

Gabriele's eyes sprung wide. "I thought you disabled the alarm?"

"I did. This is a different one. They found us."

FOUND

Gabriele shivered as Callum's eyes grew blacker. He tightened his grip on her hand and brought a finger to his lips, then he blew out the candle, throwing them into darkness.

Callum led her out of the bathroom and down the hall, and Gabriele had to hold onto his shirt to keep from stumbling. Callum navigated the darkness adeptly. They reached the end of the hall, and he slowly opened a door, pulling Gabriele inside. He carefully eased it closed again.

Callum turned on his phone for light. The room had angled ceilings that met in a peak in the middle He hurried to a desk and reached underneath with his hand, apparently for a button since a drawer suddenly popped open. He withdrew a gun.

Gabriele swallowed. She knew things were bad, but now she knew they were really bad. Callum tucked the gun into the waist of his jeans and then waved her over.

"We're over the garage," Callum whispered. He opened a hinged door on the floor behind the desk, listened, shone his light inside.

"I'll go first, then I'll help you down. It's a bit of a jump."

He disappeared before she could respond, but her instincts kicked in. With no time to think about how scared she was or that she might break a leg, she pushed herself into the hole.

Callum caught her as promised, and she was never so grateful to feel his bulging biceps around her as she was at that moment. He helped her to get steady on her feet and then opened the door to a box on wheels and motioned for her to climb inside.

"A Smart Car?" She couldn't keep the surprise from her voice.

"Great fuel mileage and a dream to park." Callum pushed the garage door button.

"Get down," he said as he got in.

He stepped on the gas and roared out of the building. The boom of gunshots was followed by a sharp crack. The back window shattered. Gabriele ducked and yelped. More shots sounded and she flinched. Callum proved to have excellent driving skills as he swerved with precision around storm debris and parked cars, and she began to see the wisdom of dodging out of a small town in a go-cart.

A tear through the dark clouds let in the dawn. Gabriele inched up in her seat and chanced a look back. She spotted headlights racing from behind. Callum had the advantage of having intimate knowledge of the village and squealed around corners into short, narrow streets. They were being chased by a dark blue vehicle that looked fast. And expensive.

"What kind of car is that?"

HEART & SOUL

Callum shifted down and spun into a narrow lane.

"A Porsche. The bastards have money to burn."

He squealed sharply around the corner of a building just past the fire hall. Gabriele gripped the door, glad she'd taken the time to put on her seatbelt. The space was tight, not meant for vehicle travel. The Smart Car barely fit through. The Porsche slammed to a stop. The hot squealing of tires filled the quiet morning air as the Porsche shifted into reverse and stepped on the pedal.

Callum maneuvered along the other side of the building, knocking into trash bins and taking out a collection of bikes in a rack.

"Sorry, mates," Callum said through tense lips.

They whisked across the main road just as the Porsche reversed into position behind them.

Callum cursed. He turned sharply down the pedestrian underground. It was like trying on a too-small cardigan. The side mirror scraped along the cement walls, removing a strip of the mural. There was no way the Porsche could follow, but the driver could figure out where they would exit from quite easily.

Callum must've had the same thought since he suddenly shifted into reverse, driving with his neck cranked and his eyes set on the cracked back window.

Gabriele's heart hammered in her chest as she gripped the door handle with white knuckles. They bumped back onto the street, knocking over a grit bin.

Gabriele spotted the Porsche ahead of them, sitting at the opening of the underground passage on the other side of the roundabout.

Callum scooted onto another side road, disappearing as the Porsche entered the ring in pursuit. Gabriele thought they had lost the vehicle, but then headlights appeared behind them, racing to catch up.

Callum drove north out of Emsworth over a grass median. He yanked on the hand brake, spinning the auto one hundred and eighty degrees, and throwing Gabriele against the door. The stern look on Callum's face grew more determined as he shifted the gear up, leaving a patch of rubber behind as he made a sharp turn. They crisscrossed through an industrial section. Gabriele had lost her bearings and had no idea where they were. She peeked through the crack under the headrest. Her eyes strained to see beyond, to the left and the right. No headlights. No revving engine. She let out several short breaths.

"I think we lost them."

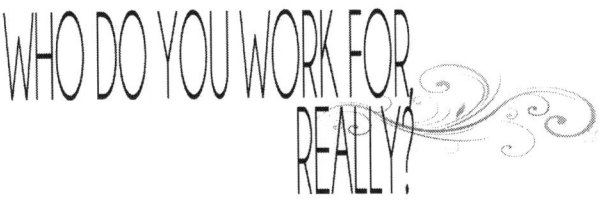

WHO DO YOU WORK FOR REALLY?

Gabriele breathed steadily through her nose. Her mind did laps around her heart, processing everything that had happened in the last twenty minutes. She and Callum had been shot at and chased.

Someone wanted to kill... *her*.

With one hand firmly on the steering wheel, Callum pressed his phone to his ear with the other. "They found us. We need a safe house." He paused. "It was too dark. I didn't see their faces." He glanced at Gabriele. "She's a little shook up, but no injuries. Yeah. Meet you there."

Gabriele frowned and held Callum with a questioning glare. This man was not a simple civil servant working on sustainability projects.

"Who do you work for, really?"

"The city."

"Yeah, right. The sustainability department." Gabriele let out an exasperated huff. "Please Callum, tell me the truth."

Callum tapped his fingers on the steering wheel, his golden brown eyes darting her way, calculating. "You're right," he finally said. "I don't work for the department of sustainability. I'm in Her Majesty's service."

"As what, her butler?"

Callum shot her a look.

"Okay, CIA?"

"That's American."

"Right, the British Secret Service?"

Callum cocked a brow. "MI5."

"Seriously?"

"They saw potential in me through the whole Sati Habib fiasco and with the skills I developed in Iraq. I was recruited last year."

Gabriele let her head fall back against the headrest. "You're a spy."

"Yes."

"And..." She peered at him sharply. "Lennon?"

"No. But I had access to secure communication lines, which was why we were able to communicate, even though technically we weren't supposed to."

Gabriele shook her head and rubbed tired eyes. "This is all so unbelievable."

Callum frowned. "Yet true."

Gabriele turned back to Callum and studied his profile. So much of what had happened over the last few days—his strange, psychotic behaviour—made sense. He'd finally answered her questions, but they only led to new ones.

"So now what?" she asked.

"I'm taking you to a safe house, and then we'll decide what to do next."

Like what flight to book her on. It was clear as day now why Callum had been so intent on sending her back to Germany as soon as possible. But that was before… the whole bathtub event. Had that changed anything at all?

Once the adrenaline rush from being shot at and chased had subsided, shivers set in—

from the cold or nerves, Gabriele wasn't sure. She'd left her cardigan behind and her feet were bare. She pulled them up and tucked them underneath her thighs.

Callum noticed and was quick to turn on the heater. Fingers of light from early dawn continued to stretch through thinning dark clouds. The sunrise was beautiful, a symbol of tranquility after the passing storm. Gabriele was still immersed in a storm of another kind and she wasn't sure she would ever find peace within it.

She cupped her eyes with her palm as if shielding them from the sun, but the reality was she didn't want Callum to see her struggle.

Callum reached over, his arm resting on her leg, and opened the glove box. He produced a pair of sunglasses and handed them to her.

She received them gratefully to shield the sun and to protect herself from Callum's scrutiny. They also gave her a way of watching Callum without being obvious.

He had a hand on the steering wheel and the other fisted over the gear shift. The stubble on his face was darker, as were the rings under his eyes. His jaw was tense, and his brow was pulled down. Gabriele could almost see the gears turning.

He had more pieces to this live-action jigsaw puzzle than she had, but by the way his eye twitched, she doubted they were fitting together.

And why did he kiss her if he planned to never see her again?

Sure, she'd kissed him back, ravenously, but he'd started it. He kissed her first.

Every few minutes, Callum's gaze flickered to the rearview mirror and more often toward Gabriele. She rested her head against the window pretending to sleep and they remained silent until they entered the outskirts of the city. Callum took an exit east onto the M25. Gabriele didn't know the area and was soon lost in a maze of brick row homes. Callum pulled the Smart Car to the curb at an end unit.

Gabriele handed the sunglasses back to Callum. "This is the safe house?"

"For now."

Callum rubbed the back of his neck as he assessed the damage to his little car. "Bollocks."

Gabriele took in the deep scratches along the black doors and the dents in the back end and shook her head. "It's pretty bad."

"Yeah, but fixable. Let's get inside."

She followed Callum to the back where he entered a code into a number pad, unlocking the door. It opened to a square, sparse kitchen with closed blinds on the windows. The air inside was stuffy.

Callum twisted the blinds open to let in a little light. Gabriele stepped through the kitchen to look around the rest of the house. The hall led to an entrance at the front of the home. On the left was a living area and on the right, a set of stairs leading up to the next floor where she assumed the bedrooms were.

When she returned to the kitchen, she found Callum sitting at the table with a laptop open and holding his phone to his ear. Gabriele didn't know where the laptop came from, but it must have been hidden away in one of the kitchen cupboards.

The counters were bare with the exception of a toaster and a knife block. There was a microwave over the stove and a washer and dryer under the counter beside a dishwasher.

A peek in the fridge was a cause for disappointment, as it contained only a selection of condiment containers and a six-pack of bottled water. She helped herself to one of the bottles and waved one in the air toward Callum, who was no longer on the phone but was studying something with intensity on his laptop.

"Sure," he said, and, "thanks," when she handed it to him.

She tried to glance at his monitor but it had a privacy shield, making it impossible to see anything unless seated directly in front of it.

Callum leaned back and smiled gently. "You must be knackered. There are a couple bedrooms upstairs. Why don't you pick one and try to sleep?"

"I don't have any of my belongings and I'd like to change out of these pajamas."

Callum reached for his phone. "I'll have something

delivered."

Gabriele wondered how that would work, considering he didn't know her size, but she was too tired to argue. After their stressful, nerve-racking, emotionally wrought night, she'd give anything to have a shower, and upon discovering the location of the loo, she took a nice, long one, letting the hot water run out.

A white robe hung on the back of the door. She sniffed it—better than the PJs that smelled of nervous sweat. She wrinkled her nose at the thought of putting those back on her body.

She checked out both rooms and selected the darkest one. She crawled under the covers and immediately fell asleep.

Gabriele awoke to the smell of something cooking. Italian? Whatever it was, it aroused her hunger. She tightened the belt of the robe around her waist and padded downstairs.

Callum was busy chopping and sautéing vegetables. He turned when he heard her, his mouth opening to speak, but when his eyes scanned her robe, nothing came out.

Gabriele crossed her arms with a sudden sense of modesty. "I don't have anything clean."

"Ah, yes." He stirred the pasta boiling in a pot on the stove. "Paula is on her way."

"Where'd the food come from?"

"Paula hit the grocery store first. She apologizes for taking so long to get you some clothes."

"Who's Paula?"

"A colleague."

"Another spy?"

"We prefer to refer to our occupation less on the nose."

"Okay, is she another *city worker*?"

"Yes."

Gabriele watched Callum stir the sauce. "I thought you didn't cook."

"I can cook. I just didn't feel like it the other night. Did you sleep?"

"Yes. Don't tell me you've been awake this whole time?"

"No. I slept on the sofa."

A bottle of wine and two glasses sat on the counter. Callum opened a drawer, removed a corkscrew and opened the bottle. Red, of course.

"Would you like a glass?" he asked.

"That would be nice." Her nerves could really use soothing right now.

He poured for both of them and then handed her one of the glasses. He tipped the edge of his to hers. "Cheers."

"Cheers."

Their eyes locked. When he finally looked away, his gaze got only as far as the patch of bare skin that formed a V on her chest. Gabriele watched his Adam's apple bounce as he swallowed.

"You look... very appealing."

Gabriele flushed red. The robe was hardly boudoir photo-worthy, but it was all that she had on. Not much of a barrier.

Callum took a step toward her and reached out to twirl a strand of her hair around his finger. It had dried in loose curls and fell along her shoulders. His touch, though not direct, made her shiver. Her pulse accelerated as he leaned close to whisper in her ear.

"You are very lovely."

His lips brushed the skin of her neck and she closed her eyes. Her blood surged and she reached to put her glass down, not trusting her fingers to retain their hold.

She whimpered a little as Callum's hand stroked her face, his fingers tilting her chin up and his mouth lightly resting on hers. She held her breath.

His lips moved over hers more urgently now, and somehow he managed to kiss her expertly while holding his wine glass and not spilling a drop.

They were in danger of repeating their performance from back at Callum's house. Gabriele hadn't been in her right mind then, and once again her body threatened to betray her.

Normally, she wasn't the kind of person to use someone else to let off steam, to wring out her emotions. Normally, she wasn't the kind of person to let someone else do that to her, either. This situation was anything but normal.

Callum's lips whispered along her neck, teasing. She whispered back along his forehead. This was wrong. They were both acting recklessly. She didn't even know how long she was staying. She'd come to England to find closure. Kissing Callum was only opening another whole can of worms.

Gabriele placed a hand on his chest and breathed out, "I don't think this is a good idea."

Callum pulled back slightly and watched her as she tried to recover. He took a short step back, releasing his hold, and let his head hang. He rubbed his eyes with his thumb and forefinger. "You're right, of course."

He looked down at her sheepishly and his lips tugged up. "I mustn't burn our dinner."

HIS BROTHER'S WIFE

Callum inhaled deeply as he turned his back on Gabriele and circled a wooden spoon through the sauce.

What was the matter with him?

He took a long drink and busied himself with meal preparation. *Stir the vegetables. Check the pasta. Is the garlic bread done?*

He couldn't believe he'd kissed her *again*. What kind of idiot was he? Had he no self-control?

Gabriele was just too damn desirable. Her honesty. Her vulnerability. Even her stubbornness—he found he wanted it all. He wanted her.

He apologized silently to Mick. Callum understood him now. He got why his brother was willing to take such big risks to be with her.

But was it more than that? He and Mick were always so competitive. When it came to sports, grades, gaining their father's attention and approval—they constantly worked to one up the other. Who had the most medals? He did. Who had the highest grades? Mick did.

Who had their father's attention?

It swayed depending on if it was time for the world cup or for university acceptance letters.

But with girls, there had always been an understanding. Girlfriends were *supposed* to be off limits. Not once in the whole time Mick was with Clover did Callum ever act inappropriately around her. And Clover was a looker. Even after Mick ended things and married Gabriele, Callum never considered that Clover could be an option for him. She was linked to Mick and always would be.

So what was the matter with him now? Gabriele wasn't just his brother's former girlfriend: she had been his wife.

Callum had been angry at Mick for risking his life for this woman. He'd warned him repeatedly not to get involved, certainly not to make it legal in any way.

Callum's eyes darted to Gabriele as she sat at the table looking like a lost child. He had blamed *her*.

But he didn't anymore. Mick was a grown man. An adult. He made his own decisions, and she didn't have anything to do with that, except that she was the incredible woman she was.

Callum wanted nothing more than to kiss her again, but giving into those impulses would be selfish and foolhardy. He and Gabriele had no future. He was toying with her feelings to satisfy his own. It had to stop. He would stop.

Callum checked the time. Where was Paula? He really needed her to buffer him. He couldn't trust himself to be alone with this beautiful woman, a woman he admired, who sat only metres away wearing nothing but a flimsy robe.

I DIDN'T MEAN TO HURT YOU

Callum had returned to his station by the stove, while Gabriele, feeling weakened by another passionate encounter, had slouched into one of the chairs. She was undeniably attracted to Callum. How could she not be? He looked like Lennon. A part of her felt like she was being unfaithful, cheating.

She wasn't though. She knew this. Lennon was dead. She was free to move on.

But with Callum? She worried he was playing with her, that she was just another thing that had belonged to his brother that he now made claim to. She hated how he'd completely disarmed her. And that he knew it.

Being alone with Callum was dangerous. She really needed some clothes.

And as if she'd summoned it, the doorbell rang.

"Wait here," Callum said. He cracked the door open, then swung it wide. He called to Gabriele, "Paula has arrived."

Paula was average height and weight and wore a navy blue pantsuit. She didn't wear makeup, and her brown hair was pulled back in a no-nonsense low ponytail.

Gabriele didn't have high hopes for the contents in the bag.

"Thanks," she said as Paula handed it to her.

"I'm Paula by the way." She extended her hand.

Gabriele shook it. "I'm Gabriele."

Paula glanced around settling her gaze on the table set for two with an opened wine bottle sitting in the middle. Her eyes cut to Callum, and her lips turned down slightly like she disapproved. "I can smell dinner, so I won't keep you."

"Would you like to join us?" Gabriele said suddenly.

Callum jumped in. "Yes, great idea. Paula, I doubt you've eaten in a while."

She cocked her head. "That's true and certainly nothing home cooked." She glanced at Gabriele, to the table and back to Callum. Her eyes were intelligent, but one didn't need advanced powers of discernment to pick up the romantic tension in the room. "If you don't mind," she said politely, "I'll accept your invitation."

Gabriele left Callum with Paula in the kitchen and skipped upstairs feeling relieved that she and Callum wouldn't be left alone. They needed time to diffuse their mutual attraction. Gabriele determined to keep her distance from Callum from now on. No more touching!

Gabriele opened the shopping bag and began to remove the items one by one: small bikini panties, a black B-cup bra, a pair of straight-leg, low-waist jeans, a long-sleeved blue and white striped blouse, a dark knit cardigan, a thin black synthetic bomber jacket, socks and a pair of trainers in her shoe size.

Gabriele chuckled. How did Paula know?

She dressed quickly and used the brush she found on the cupboard in the loo to brush her hair. She wished she had makeup, but having nice, new clothes that fit just right made up for it.

Callum regarded her appreciatively when she joined them. Gabriele smiled at him and quickly turned her attention to Paula. "These are great. How did you... ?"

"Callum sent me a couple photos, and I was able to establish your size and style from that."

Gabriele eyed Callum as she took the seat across from him, wondering what pictures he had of her and why he had them?

Callum jumped up to retrieve her unfinished glass of wine from the counter and handed it to her.

"Thanks."

"*Bon Appétit*," Callum said, taking his chair. "Dig in."

Callum had prepared spaghetti with stir-fried vegetables on the side and toasted garlic bread. Gabriele almost inhaled her meal, not realizing just how hungry she was.

"This is amazing," she said.

He winked. "I'm glad you like it."

"So, Gabriele, " Paula began as she tore her bread in two. "Is this your first time to London?"

Gabriele shook her head and dabbed her mouth with a paper serviette. "No. I studied here for a semester three years ago as part of my language studies."

"That explains your excellent grasp of English. Do you speak any other languages besides German?"

"I'm fluent in French, Italian and Spanish."

Callum cut in, "Any Arab nation languages?"

Gabriele considered him. "I studied Arabic for a year as an elective, but I wouldn't say I could converse in it."

"Can you read it?" he asked.

"To a degree."

Paula cleared her voice. "I'm sorry your visit this time around was so... unpleasant."

Gabriele's eye caught Callum's. "It hasn't been *all* bad. But getting shot at and chased this morning was a low point."

Paula smirked. "Your attitude commends you."

"Thanks. But I still don't understand why they want *me* so badly?"

Callum lowered his fork. "They think you know what Mick knew. Otherwise, you wouldn't have come back. And now that you're with me... well, now you do know." His lips pulled down into that scowl he continually wore when they first met. "I've made things worse for you."

Gabriele now wished she was sitting closer to Callum. She really wanted to reach out and touch him, to let him know she didn't blame him. "I'm glad I know."

"And," Callum added with a sigh, "it seems our friend Sati Habib has taken a particular interest in you. You were, after all, the wife of the man who betrayed him, the reason he spent almost two years in prison."

Gabriele lost her breath. "He's not still in prison?"

Callum and Paula exchanged a look before he answered. "No. He was released two days ago."

Two days ago? So those times she felt like she was being followed and it wasn't Callum... it was... Sati?

Gabriele's forehead grew damp and she patted at it with her serviette.

HEART&SOUL

"I'm sorry," Callum said quietly.

Paula pushed away from the table, having eaten in record time. This lady didn't mess around. "Thanks for the meal, Callum," she said as she donned her blazer. "I owe you." She turned to Gabriele. "Nice to meet you."

"Likewise."

Gabriele watched Paula as she briskly walked to the kitchen door, carefully locking it before closing it behind her.

Callum studied Gabriele from across the table with a warm, intense gaze that made her squirm. Why did he insist on staring at her like that? She felt pinned to her chair under some kind of soul-searching examination. She really hoped his spy training hadn't included some kind of high-tech/science-fiction mind-reading skills. She'd be mortified if he knew how scrambled and confused her emotions were right now, particularly regarding him. The attraction she felt was undeniable, but was it trustworthy?

Was he trustworthy?

She stared back without smiling. "When's my flight?"

Guilt flashed behind his eyes. "Nine-fifteen tomorrow morning."

So, she was right. It was already booked. Callum was just playing with her like a heartless lion toying with the antelope it fully intends to kill.

She blinked back hot tears, feeling foolish and small. She gathered her dishes and began to clear away the meal, keeping her head down and her eyes averted.

"Gabriele?"

"I'm fine." *You win.* "It's time I left. I'll sell the cottage. I won't come back."

"Gabi?"

She pinched her eyes closed at the use of her pet name. The name her closest friends and family called her. What Lennon had called her. She felt his hand on her shoulder and she tensed.

"I didn't mean to hurt you."

What did he mean to do then? She pulled away from his touch. "I said I'm fine."

A KNOCK ON THE DOOR

There was a sharp tap on the kitchen door. Gabriele shot Callum a look.

"It's probably Paula." He checked his phone. "We have security posted on the street. They would've called if it were someone else."

Gabriele peeked out the window but couldn't see anyone in the dark. Callum flicked the switch for the outside light, but it didn't come on.

"I told someone to change that bulb," he muttered.

Still, he opened the door cautiously. "Paula?" He glanced back at Gabriele as he began to shut the door. "No one there."

Then the door was kicked open, knocking Callum backwards, and a strange young man in dark clothing filled the entrance.

Gabriele froze.

"Sati," Callum said, moving into a fighting stance.

This was the man who was responsible for all the terrible things that had happened to Lennon. He had black hair shaved short, a dark beard on caramel skin and black as night eyes devoid of soul. His gaze stayed on Gabriele for a long moment, and the hatred she saw there made her insides shrivel.

He refocused on Callum taking sure steps towards him. He wielded a knife.

Gabriele screamed.

Callum kicked Sati sharply in the center of his chest. It was enough to knock him backwards, but not off his feet. The man's face was hard with steely, inhuman eyes. He lunged at Callum with the knife again.

Callum held his fists up and in front of his face, legs wide and bent slightly at the knees. The attacker swung, but Callum stepped in and blocked his arm with his left wrist and swiftly elbowed him in the face with his right. The knife fell with a clang. Sati stumbled back, but returned with a fist strike to Callum's face. The blow caused Callum to collapse to the floor.

It all happened so fast, in seconds. Gabriele couldn't believe her eyes.

Sati retrieved the knife and held it above Callum, preparing to strike. Callum kicked his hand with one foot, and the man's groin with the other in quick succession, momentarily disabling him. Callum hopped back to his feet.

The attacker recovered, growled and sliced through the air with the knife.

Callum dodged, dipping under his arm and striking Sati in the kidney with his the heel of his left hand. Sati yelled, spun and returned with a sharp elbow-punch to Callum's face, knocking him to the floor. He lay there dazed as the man hovered over him, knife in hand.

Gabriele had no doubt he would kill Callum. "Stop!" she yelled. Impulsively, she jumped on the attacker's back.

He flung around, dropping the knife, and pulled her off his back with two strong arms. He squeezed her to his chest, holding her tight with an arm wrapped around her neck. Gabriele gagged for breath.

Callum clumsily worked his way to his feet. "Let her go."

"My mission is to kill you both. I might as well start with her." His grip tightened.

Gabriele eyed the corkscrew on the nearby counter. If she could just grab it.

"Sati, she's innocent," Callum said. "Let her go and I'll surrender myself to you."

Gabriele reached slowly, her fingers clasping the pen-like cork remover.

"She is not innocent! None who are not on the side of Allah are innocent."

Gabriele opened the little knife used for removing the foil around the cork and with a sharp stroke, stabbed her attacker in the thigh.

Sati bellowed and loosened his grip. Gabriele sent her elbow straight back into his solar plexus and he buckled over. She stepped backwards and followed through with a karate chop to the back of his neck. Sati collapsed to the floor. He groaned, pressing a hand on the wound on his leg. Blood spurted between his thick fingers.

Gabriele scooted behind Callum who flashed her a look of disbelief. Then he knelt to the ground and pulled on Sati's shirt. He punched him in the jaw and knocked him out.

He grabbed Gabriele's hand. "Let's go."

A FLOWER AT DUSK

Gabriele's fingers shook as she worked her seatbelt closed. She'd wasted precious seconds by going to the wrong side of the Smart Car. Callum just pushed her to crawl over the stick shift to the passenger seat.

Callum started the car and drove off. Then he flipped open his phone. "Need security and a cleanup crew at safe house eight. Suspect is down and unconscious, but could come to at any time. Proceed with caution. Security unaccounted for."

Callum lay his phone down and reached over for Gabriele's hand. "Are you all right?"

Was she all right? She'd almost been killed and she'd just stabbed someone.

"I think so."

"You did good. Really good. Most untrained women would've screamed bloody murder with no sense of how to fight back. Where'd you learn to fight like that?"

HEART & SOUL

"I took a self-defense class."

"That's good. Every girl should take one. Though, jumping on his back wasn't a great idea."

"It saved your life."

"It did. I should thank you for that."

She tilted her head. "I'm waiting."

Callum smirked. "Thank you."

"I should thank you as well. I'm losing count of how many times you've saved my life in the last day."

He cocked a brow. "I'm waiting."

She couldn't help but allow a slight smile. "Thank you."

He patted her leg in a way that was too familiar and intimate. Gabriele felt herself close up like a flower at dusk. She had to protect her heart from this man. Sure, he'd saved her life, but at the same time it felt like he was slowly killing her, too.

They approached the city center within twenty-five minutes. The lights on the turreted Tower Bridge reflected off the River Thames. The cabbie had been right. It was breathtaking at night. Was that taxi ride really only six days ago?

Callum drove through congested traffic past the massive St. Paul's Cathedral and further along the north side of the Thames. He pulled into a secure car park in a limestone building.

"Thames House," Callum announced. "Where the highly secure offices of the secret service are. Also known as the grid."

"What are we going to do here?"

"I'm going to work. You're going to wait."

Right. Wait until morning when she and Callum would say goodbye and never see each other again.

Why did he have to kiss her? Why did he have to make her want him?

She hated him now. If she could leave right this moment, she would.

Callum sighed and Gabriele matched it, releasing a frustrated breath of her own. Callum eyed her carefully. He wouldn't be much of a spy if he couldn't detect the cold feelings she vented toward him.

She followed him through a security check, much like what you had to go through at an airport. She was clean, with only the clothes on her back. Callum passed through without presenting his gun. She knew he had one, but he must've left it in the car.

They went through another automated scanner before entering the grid. Gabriele was surprised by the number of people working there, most of them staring intently at their computer monitors.

"Callum." Paula waved them over. "Hello, Gabriele. Good to see you again. Sorry it's under poor circumstances. Shurooq will take you to a room where you can rest."

A slender, olive-skinned girl with long dark hair greeted her with a smile. Gabriele smiled back, then glanced questioningly at Callum.

"Go with her. I need to attend this meeting. I'll check in on you later."

Shurooq led her past a number of occupied desks and down a short hallway where she opened a door to what looked like a guest room. There was a cot prepared along the wall, a side table with a lamp and a comfortable chair in the corner. It lacked natural light, so the atmosphere came off more clinical than cozy. A bathroom with a shower stall was off to the side.

The girl opened the drawer in the side table and removed a thin mid-sized case. "You'll find a toothbrush and toiletries in here along with a large T-shirt for sleeping." She handed

Gabriele the case. "It's similar to what the airlines hand out when they lose your luggage."

"Thank you... Shurooq. That's an interesting name."

The girl's dark eyes held hers. "It's Muslim."

Gabriele kept her expression staid, but inside her stomach swirled. "Forgive me, but I find it surprising that a Muslim would work for the British Secret Service."

"Why is that?"

"It feels... incongruous. Aren't most of the terrorists plotting against Great Britain in the 21st Century Muslim?"

"They are."

Gabriele lowered herself on the cot. Shurooq appeared to change her mind about leaving and settled into the chair. "Tell me exactly what is bothering you."

"Well, for one, I almost had my neck broken tonight by someone who is most certainly Muslim, and, let's not forget being shot at earlier today by the same guy.

"Plus, and this is a big one, my husband had to flee the country because of something he found on his Muslim roommate's computer, and *he was killed anyway.*"

Gabriele breathed sharply through the heat of anger that assaulted her.

"I'm truly sorry, Gabriele. Not all Muslims are like that. I'm not like that. Most Muslims follow a religion of peace, mercy and forgiveness, and the majority have nothing to do with the extremely grave events which have come to be associated with our faith."

Gabriele stared hard at the girl. "I'm a Christian. My parents are pastors of a street church in Dresden. I confess I don't know that much about the Islamic faith, only that it scares me. If a Muslim says or does something that is offensive to me as a Christian, I may get mad, but I wouldn't consider for a moment that I had the right to kill that person because of it. However, if I offend Muslims, and I have apparently by marrying someone they consider an infidel, then my life is in danger." Her voice dropped to a whisper. "I've never been hunted before."

"This is why I work for MI5," Shurooq said carefully. "Because I'm against extreme Islam for the same reasons you are. Everyone should be free to live their lives and practice their beliefs without fear."

She stood to leave. "Is there anything else you need?"

Gabriele shook her head. "No."

Shurooq held her gaze for a moment before stepping out the door. "Rest well, Ms Baumann."

SAFE AND SECURE

Paula shot Callum a look. "You look like hell. Why don't you go clean up a bit before we start?"

Callum had a spare set of clean clothes in a locker in the men's room. He grabbed a fresh shirt and stood in front of the mirror. His shirt sleeve was streaked with blood from his nose and there was some caked in the bristles on his chin. He washed his face with cold water, wincing as his hands moved over the bruising on his jaw. He dried his face then donned the clean shirt. His abs burned as he stretched his arms out from the beating he took. Callum knew from experience that he was going to be stiff and sore for some time.

At least Sati Habib was behind bars again. That meant Gabriele was safe. The cell group didn't care about her. From the intel they'd gathered, she had been a personal vendetta, a revenge mark for Sati.

Maybe it would be okay if she stayed in Emsworth? If she still wanted to, that was.

The others were seated around the table in the meeting room when Callum caught up to them. It was a dull, sparse room and soundproof—fully secure when the door was closed. Paula Tate, Shurooq Massoud and their senior case officer, Joe Langstone were the lone occupants. The room was windowless with central air keeping it ventilated. It was lit with unflattering florescent lighting that reflected off Joe's bald head.

"What'd I miss?" Callum asked as he pulled out a chair.

Joe answered. "Sati Habib isn't talking."

"Not surprising, there," Callum said. It wasn't unlike the extremists to get tightlipped under custody. They knew the British law protected them from human rights abuses such as torture tactics to gain cooperation.

"Agent Rebani is working on the inside. He has a wire, but most of the conversations are ambiguous," Shurooq said. "The cell leader, Musa Fayad, is cocky and talks in broad strokes. Vague references to "the next imminent operation. We have every reason to believe something big is going to drop soon."

"Do we know in what form the attack is coming?" Paula asked.

Shurooq shook her head. "Not exactly, but Rebani presumes it'll be another bomb."

Joe tented his fingers over his belly. "And the target?"

Shurooq answered, "Just that it's a travel hub."

"That could be bridges, tubes, buses," Callum said. "Airports."

"We need more information," Paula said. "We need specifics."

"Agreed," Joe said. "In the meantime, put out a high-security alert for all of London with particular attention to transit hubs. Callum, return Ms Baumann to Germany as soon as possible, then see me for further instructions."

Callum had let hope rise for a moment, that maybe there was a chance that Gabriele could stay, but Joe squashed it firmly with his words.

And he was right. Gabriele would never be safe with Callum. There was a very real chance he may not make it home from work one day. Agents died on the field all the time. The last thing Gabriele needed was to have another guy she cared for die on her. It wasn't fair of him to ask it of her. Best if she went back to Germany and met a nice, stable German man whose job was safe and secure. But was Germany the safest place?

"They could find her there, too," Callum said. "Just as easily as they found Mick."

Joe tapped the table with a thick forefinger. "She doesn't qualify for our protection."

"And even if she did," Paula said, "she would have to give up all ties to her family and friends. Disappear from their lives forever. Do you think she'd agree to that?"

Callum shook his head. He knew Gabriele would be too stubborn to even consider something like that.

"What's the next best option?" he asked.

"She should choose a different country and stay under the radar for a while," Joe said. "Ask her what she thinks about Canada or Brazil."

Callum ground his teeth together, feeling helpless. They were right, of course. Germany was out of the question for now, yet he doubted she'd be willing to leave Europe entirely. He'd figure out a way to broach the subject with her tomorrow.

They moved onto the next item of the agenda—ensuring sufficient security detail for the duration of the Israeli Prime Minister's visit—but Gabriele Baumann remained on Callum's mind.

I'M NOT KISSING YOU GOODBYE

Gabriele awoke to music from the clock radio on the side table, telling her is was 07:00. Shurooq must have set it. She sat up and turned on the light. On the floor by the door were all her things she'd left behind in the cottage and at Callum's house: her suitcase and carry-on bag, her makeup kit and purse. Someone had retrieved the objects and delivered them here.

There was no mistaking the message. She was leaving England for good.

A sigh released from her lungs, long and slow. It failed to remove the burden of heavy emotion that had settled on her chest.

The old adage was true. Ignorance is bliss. Meeting Clover, knowing that "Mick Leatherby" could've had a long life with her had he not stumbled across the Al Qaeda, had he not had to flee and leave her behind broken-hearted: knowing the truth about Lennon didn't ease the pain.

Gabriele couldn't help but feel like she had been a reconciliation prize.

But that wasn't fair. Lennon treated her well. Showered her with adoration. He'd hid a large piece of himself from her, but she understood why now. Having been a target herself made Lennon's motives clear. She'd have to do the same thing to protect her own family and she wouldn't hesitate to lie by omission to do it.

And now there was Callum.

Callum who looked like Lennon, but was nothing like him. Callum was his own person, and though they shared some traits—like how to enamour a woman—his approach to life was completely opposite. When it came to fight or flight, Lennon was a runner. Callum was a fighter.

Both aspired to peacekeeping, but from opposite sides of the coin.

Gabriele showered and put on fresh clothes, her own clothes, leaving the ones Paula had purchased folded on the cot after she made it. She carefully applied makeup and blow-dried her hair. If Callum was so intent on saying good-bye, she wanted to burn an impression of herself on his mind.

She answered a tap on the door, expecting to see him, but it was Shurooq on the other side of the knock. She held a tray with breakfast.

"Good morning," she said cheerily, laying the tray down on the side table. "I imagine you must be hungry. It's not much, just a couple croissants with butter and jam and a cup of coffee with foamed milk."

Gabriele smiled. She obviously got her instructions from Callum. "It's great, thanks."

"You have fifteen minutes before Callum arrives to collect you."

She left as dutifully as she arrived.

Gabriele ate quickly, brushed her teeth and added lip colour to her lips. She zipped up her bags and when she turned around Callum was standing in the doorway. Her heart tumbled down a long hill.

He wore trousers instead of jeans, a shirt, tie and suit jacket, looking nothing like a former soldier and everything like a government agent. His face was an assortment of bruises. Bluish-green spots peppered his jaw and cheekbone.

It didn't take away from his good looks. In fact, to her chagrin, she found him more appealing than ever.

His eyes appraised her as she stood there like a dazed deer. "Good morning," he finally said.

"Good morning." She turned her back to him, reaching for her suitcase, unsure how she was going to get through the twenty-minute ride to London City Airport. She inhaled and mentally challenged herself to be strong.

There were fewer security measures when it came to leaving the Thames House and before long Callum had them driving through the city, this time in a classic, dark blue sedan.

"Where do you really live?" Gabriele asked. "You're not in Emsworth. You can't have spent the night at the Thames House last night."

"I have a flat in the city."

Gabriele wondered what it would be like to live in a city like London. "Is it nice?"

Callum glanced at her. "Pretty nice."

"I moved back in with my parents when Lennon died. Never moved out again. Pretty pathetic."

"It's not pathetic, Gabi. It's understandable."

She swallowed. There he was using her pet name again.

"It's why I came to England to see the cottage," she continued. "I needed a push to get out of Dresden. To get away from my parents. They're dear, don't get me wrong, but they will care for me for their whole lives if I let them. I had to push myself out of the nest."

"Speaking of leaving the nest," Callum began, "Germany is no longer safe for you. It's our consensus that you should settle somewhere else, at least for a while."

Gabriele was stunned. "Like where?"

"Canada and Brazil were suggested."

" You're kidding, right?"

"Unfortunately, no. Take a couple days to think about it. Choose a place you'd like to live. You can tell your parents you got a job in Greece or Japan. We'll arrange it, so it will be true. We can give you a new ID." He shot her an apologetic glance. "But other than that, you'd be on your own."

The news just kept getting worse and worse. "You really think I'm not safe in Dresden?"

"You could put your family in danger as well."

Oh, God. She had no choice then. She had to keep her distance from home for the sake of those she loved. She began to understand Lennon in a deeper way.

"I need a day to process."

"Paula will be in touch."

Gabriele felt her throat grow thick with emotion. She opened up the glove box, hoping Callum had moved the extra pair of sunglasses he had stashed in the Smart Car over. Good.

He had. She put them on because she didn't want him to see her eyes, the anguish that was building there.

She also wanted to look at him. She shifted slightly in her seat so she could face him and watch his profile without being obvious. The truth was that she wanted to burn his image on her mind, too. This was Callum's profile, not Lennon's. She wasn't confusing the two.

"I can tell you're looking at me." He was so full of himself.

"I'm not kissing you good-bye."

The corner of his mouth tugged up as if he acknowledged the challenge and would rise to it.

Callum's phone chimed. He checked it and answered. "Hi, Paula."

His face grew stern and his gaze darted to the rearview mirror.

"Yes, there's been a white van behind us for the last mile or so… What should I do? I'm on it."

He hung up and glanced at Gabriele with a look that was hard to discern.

"What's wrong?"

"The passenger in the van behind us is a suicide bomber. The driver has instructions to follow us to the LCY where he'll drop off the bomber who will follow us to the check-in line."

A heavy flush of fear filled Gabriele's chest. The lobby of the London City Airport was vast and bustling with people coming and going. There were long check-in lines, a busy restaurant, car hire booths, a book store, and other customer services. It wasn't a huge airport like Gatwick, but an explosion could kill hundreds of people.

She swallowed. "What are you supposed to do now?"

He looked at her again with something close to regret. "Run him off the road."

"Won't that set the bomb off?"

"Maybe. There's a good chance it's on a timer to line up with your check-in time. I'm going to stop to let you out."

Callum signaled to pull to the shoulder, but instead of slowing down, the van rammed them in the back. Gabriele's neck jerked back against the headrest. She cried out, "What are they doing?"

"They don't want me to stop. They don't want me to let you out."

Gabriele didn't understand. "I thought getting rid of me was personal to Sati?"

Callum grimaced. "I thought so, too."

Obviously Sati's reach extended beyond the prison walls. That meant she'd never be safe. Callum was right. They'd follow her to Germany and she'd bring danger to her family.

THE CHASE

Callum hit the accelerator. When the opposing lane was free, he crossed it and slammed on the brakes. The van was too big to match his maneuver in time and ended up alongside a car.

Callum cranked the steering wheel, slamming the car into the side of the van. The side windows shattered, spraying glass. Gabriele screamed.

Callum turned the steering wheel sharply to right the car.

The van sped up as if it were now trying to outrun Callum rather than decommission him.

Paula's voice crackled from the speaker phone. "Status?"

"We're on A1261 heading into the roundabout at Leamouth," he shouted. "Suspect is aggressive."

It was Callum's mandate to run the van off the road to avoid an explosion in a populated area, but now Callum was confused as to what the bombers intention was. Were they rushing ahead to complete their operation at a peak time? If so, did they still care if Gabriele was in the airport? Or had their instructions changed? What was their priority? Killing Gabriele or making a bigger statement by killing hundreds or thousands at LCY?

The van didn't slow down as it approached the circle. Attempting to keep up, Callum pressed down on the accelerator, inertia practically pulling the car up on two wheels. Gabriele whimpered, and Callum cursed himself for not being able to spare her this. He had to force the van off the road before it reached the airport at any cost.

Even if it meant his life. And hers.

At least they were out of the heavily populated area of the city, and the motorists on the motorway had the good sense to pull over and get out of the way of the speedsters.

There was a tree-lined stretch just before the next roundabout. If he could just force them off the road there.

He shifted into high gear and pulled up beside the van once again. This time the driver twisted in his seat to point a gun out the window.

Callum shouted, "Get down!" just as the shot was fired. The bullet pierced the window. Gabriele shrieked and wrapped her arms over her head.

They approached a construction zone. Callum pressed on his horn repeatedly to warn the crew to jump out of the way of the van bearing down on them. Orange road markers blew clumsily across the road, and Callum swerved to miss the bigger barrels.

Something that looked like construction wire caught in the

back wheel of the van. Callum had the advantage he was looking for. The van slowed, and Callum knocked the car into the ailing wheel. The tire flattened causing the van to circle violently, clipping the side of the car and sending them both into the ditch.

The sudden expansion of the airbag smacked Callum in the face. Dark circles muddied his vision until he blacked out.

SOMETHING SHE'D NEVER DREAMED SHE'D DO

Gabriele's breath was tight in her throat. Through the broken glass of her window, she could see the van pressed up against the back of their car. The driver and passenger of the van were slumped forward unconscious, possibly dead.

Callum groaned. Gabriele nudged his shoulder. "Callum? Are you all right?"

He blinked. "I think so." He looked at her carefully. "Are you?"

"Yeah, I'm okay."

Callum's hand searched the seat. "Where's my phone?"

Gabriele spotted it on the floor. "Here."

Their fingers brushed as he took it from her. His bronze eyes bore into her with something like remorse. "I'm so sorry."

"It's not your fault."

HEART & SOUL

Callum wrenched the banged-up door open and slid out of the car. His phone was to his ear and Gabriele could hear him reporting back. Mission accomplished. Suspects are injured, possibly fatally. She heard sirens in the distance.

Gabriele watched through the shattered back window as Callum cautiously approached the van. The driver's head suddenly popped up, and he shook it as if to clear his vision. Then his eyes locked on Callum. Callum turned and dashed for the car, but the driver was fast. Callum's hand slipped under the seat. The van driver grabbed Callum's shoulder, pulling him away from the car and right hooked him in the face.

"Callum!"

Callum fell to the ground, pushing back on his heels. Blood gushed from his nose. The driver kicked him in the side and Callum yelled out. He pulled a gun out of his pocket and aimed it.

Oh, God, he's going to kill him.

Gabriele reached under the driver's seat. *Where is it? Where is it?* Callum had been after his gun, she was sure of it.

Her fingers grasped the cool handle of the weapon and pulled it free. Then she didn't something she'd never dreamed she'd do in a million years. She aimed through the open door and pulled the trigger.

GRAVEL CRUNCHING UNDER FOOTSTEPS

The gun kicked back, wrenching her wrist. She cried out and tossed the weapon. Her breath came in short, loud spurts. Her heart thundered wildly. Her eyes searched beyond the open door to the street for Callum. She couldn't see him. The man she shot had fallen on top of him.

"Callum!" Gabriele's fingers felt like thick sausages as she worked feverishly to undo her seatbelt. It clicked open, and she scrambled to get out of the vehicle, crawling over the stick shift and out the driver's door. The broken glass bit her palms, but at that moment she didn't notice the pain. She needed to get to Callum.

The fallen man groaned, gripping his leg. Blood soaked through the denim. He was out of Callum's reach, but his gun lay on the ground nearby. Gabriele scurried along the rough surface of asphalt and pushed the man's gun far out of reach, then hurried to Callum's side.

HEART&SOUL

Blood soaked Callum's right shoulder and her heart plummeted. "Callum!"

She pressed two fingers against his neck, grateful to find a pulse. It was slight but present. She ripped off her cardigan and pressed it against the blood flow from Callum's shoulder. He moaned.

"Callum." He was losing blood. He had to get to a hospital. Where was the ambulance? Weren't the sirens she'd heard earlier for them? She needed to find his phone, call the grid, but she didn't know where it was. She hated the thought of leaving his side. She stroked his head and a lump formed in her throat. "I'll be right back. I'm just going to find your phone."

He licked dry lips. "They'll find us."

Gabriele glanced at the man she'd shot. He writhed on the ground, and she felt bad that she hadn't tried to help him. She didn't have any nursing training, only basic first aid, but something told her he was too dangerous to approach, even in his injured state.

She glanced back at the van and her pulse jumped. The passenger seat was empty. She thought the guy had died, but obviously he'd come to. Her heart hammered. They were in grave danger. She scrambled back toward the car, looking for the gun she'd dropped. It lay on the ground under the vehicle. She must've kicked it when she let it go. She bent low, reaching. Her fingers just brushed the edge of the metal when she heard the gravel crunch beside her. Her heart pattered as she clawed for the gun. Sharp pain ripped along her ribs and she cried out. In a flash strong arms pulled her out from under the vehicle, and the skin of her arms burned as it scraped along the rough, glass-ridden surface. She yelled, "No!"

Pain exploded in her head and her world blackened.

TELL ME SOMETHING I DON'T KNOW

Gabriele first became aware of the pounding in her head—she'd never had a headache so fierce before—then the musky smell of cool dampness. The rusty taste of blood in her mouth and the cramping in her lower back were next. Her eyes flickered open to a dim swirl of light. She squinted at the source, a small window high above her. She tried to move her arms, but they were trapped behind her back. She noted that she was sitting on a wobbly, wooden chair. Her hands prickled from lack of circulation as she tried to move them.

A whoosh of blood flooded her as her memory returned.

"Callum?" she muttered. Her throat was dry, her mouth thick with a puffy tongue. She'd die for a drink of water right now.

Probably a bad choice of words.

"Callum?" she repeated, fighting the panic. She couldn't see him. Was she alone in this dark room?

"Gabi."

His voice was low and muffled, but it meant he was alive and with her. It came from directly behind her. She twisted her head and yelped at the pain that seared through her scalp.

"Are you okay?" Callum asked.

"My head is killing me." Her eyes had adjusted and she could see the duct tape wrapped around her chest and around her ankles. "And I'm tied up."

"Me, too."

Gabriele felt Callum's fingers wiggle against hers. Their situation crystalized. They were tied together with the same tape, back to back in some kind of cellar. She'd fallen into a badly written noir movie.

She remembered shooting one of their pursuers to save Callum. She remembered the blood. "How's your shoulder?"

"It's been better. They had the decency at least to bandage it up."

"They must mean to let us live then."

"For now."

Gabriele shivered at his words. "Why do you think we're still alive?" She remembered one of the men standing over Callum, ready to shoot.

"Leverage, I imagine. They want something. They think they can bargain with our lives to get it."

"Can they?"

A pause, then, "No. The British government doesn't negotiate with terrorists."

He was being brutally honest, and Gabriele appreciated that. She swallowed thickly. There had to be a way for them to escape. She shuffled in her chair and pulled on the tape. Callum groaned.

"Sorry," she said.

"It's fine. Just my shoulder."

She pushed down her growing anxiety. "What are we going to do?"

"There's nothing we can do. Just wait."

Just wait? For what? For the terrorists to come back and kill them?

"I'm so sorry." Callum's voice was hoarse and labored. He'd lost a lot of blood, and Gabriele worried he might pass out.

"It's okay. Just rest."

"It's not okay." His voice cracked. "You shouldn't be here with me. It was my job to protect you and I failed."

"You tried, Callum. You did everything in your power to get rid of me. It's not your fault I'm so stubborn."

She heard him snort. "That you are."

"Hey. You don't have to agree with me."

"Okay, fine. You're a pushover."

She filled her lungs with damp, moldy air. "We're going to die, aren't we?"

"I don't know."

Callum's fingers brushed against hers again, and she wiggled hers back. She needed to touch him, to feel his skin on hers even if it was just their fingertips.

"I'm not afraid of death," she said. "I'm not crazy about pain or the thought of going through the act of dying, but I'm not afraid of what comes next."

"That's good."

"Are you?"

"I try not to think about it. If there's something on the

other side, I'll find out about it when I get there."

"I believe there is something on the other side. Heaven. My grandparents are there. And Lennon. I'm just sad for the pain that my... dying here... will cause my family. I wish I could see them one more time."

Callum shifted and Gabriele felt his hand grasp her fingers. She twisted her wrists until her hand could reach to clasp it back. They sat quietly in the growing darkness, holding hands behind their backs. She tilted her head, leaning it against the back of Callum's head. It was the most awkward yet intense kind of intimacy.

"Can you believe we've only known each other for one week?" she whispered.

"No."

"I feel like I've known you... for at least two," she joked.

"I wish I'd known you for much, much longer."

Gabriele was sure he was growing delirious. The funny thing was, she felt the same way. She didn't have any regrets with how she'd lived her life, but she did regret that she wouldn't have the chance to really get to know Callum Leatherby.

Suddenly, she desperately needed to know more about him. Something, anything before she died.

"Tell me something I don't know about you."

"What?" Callum responded with surprise.

"Please, just something. Talk to me."

A pause, then, "I'm allergic to plums."

"Plums? Any other fruits?"

"Nope, just plums."

"That's so random. I don't think I'm allergic to anything."

The room was like a mausoleum. The low ceiling and

nearby walls lined with empty shelves deadened the sound. All Gabriele could hear was the beat of her own heart and Callum's raspy breathing behind her. She was afraid if he passed out, he might never wake up. She had to keep him talking.

"Have you ever been in love?"

"Gabi, seriously?"

"Humor me. We might die here. What can it hurt?"

She heard him take in a long, slow breath. "Yes. Briefly. When I was thirteen. Does that count? It might've been infatuation, but damn, she had the cutest black pigtails and a fashionable bright pink Spice Girls rucksack."

"I'm serious."

"No, I haven't. That was Mick's department. He was romantic enough for the both of us."

Gabriele felt both relieved and disappointed. For some reason she was glad Callum didn't have ghosts of girlfriends past for her to compete with but on the other hand, it showed that Callum wasn't interested in falling in love.

The question was, was she?

Gabriele ran her tongue along dry lips. She missed Lennon. But she also missed being in love: the blissful euphoria that came with discovering all there was to know about a person you admired and desired, the hope of experiencing life and witnessing life with someone you loved and who loved you in return, growing old together.

Was she in love with Callum? What were these confusing emotions that bit at her heart?

Not that it mattered. Chances were good they'd both be dead by morning.

HEART & SOUL

"Tell me something I don't know about you," Callum said softly.

She exhaled a small scoff. "Is there anything you don't know?"

He qualified, "Tell me something Mick didn't know about you."

Gabriele sucked in a breath. Callum wanted something she hadn't given to Lennon. Why?

She'd shared a lot with Lennon, but not everything. Maybe she would've over time, but they'd run out of that.

"When I was fifteen, I dated a man who was twenty-five. I told my parents that he was twenty and they still freaked out about that. He was charming and generous and made me feel like I was a mature woman and not the silly girl I really was. Girls that age just want to be treated like adults, you know. Always in a hurry to grow up. Of course he wanted more from me than I was willing or ready to give. One day he threw a party at his flat, and after I'd had a couple beers, he pushed me into an empty bedroom. I fought him, but I was in a weakened state having been drinking, and he was twice my size. If one of his drunken friends hadn't stumbled in with a girl in his arms, something awful would've happened. I got away and ran home. I never told anyone. I was too embarrassed."

"We have to escape, Gabi, so I can hunt down and kill that guy."

Gabriele's lips pulled up into a slight smile. "He was a creep, but it made me determined never to let myself get into a compromising situation again. I'd wanted to grow up and I did. I got smarter and stronger. That's when I took the self-defense class."

Callum squeezed her fingers. "Thanks for telling me that."

Gabriele squeezed back. "It felt confessional."

"I have a confession, too," Callum said. "Mick and I shared everything, but never girls. We had an unspoken agreement. I broke it once."

Gabriele's stomach clenched. "With Clover?"

"No, not her."

Gabriele sighed with an undefinable relief.

"It was the girl he was with just before Clover. Alice Bentley. They stayed together for only three months, and somewhere in the middle of that time, I kissed her. The three of us were watching the telly. Well, I was trying to watch. Mick and Alice were playing tongue wars, and it was ticking me off that they would make out with me sitting right there. They thought they were being discreet because the room was dark, but a telly sheds a lot more light than you'd think. I tried to ignore them, but, being the young hormonal twit that I was, I was also fascinated and my eyes were on them more often than they were on the movie we were all supposedly watching.

"During an advert, Mick skipped upstairs to the loo. I got it in my head that I wanted to know what it was like to kiss Alice, too, so I scooted close to her, leaned in and kissed her. Her eyes bugged out at first, but then she closed them and kissed me back. We broke apart when we heard the stairs creak. I put a finger to my lips indicating that she shouldn't tell Mick. I stood quickly and said I wasn't feeling well, and I went to bed. It wasn't a lie. I felt sick over what I did. After that, I vowed never to touch one of Mick's girls. And I hadn't. Until yesterday."

It seemed like forever and a day ago that Gabriele had made out with Callum in the bathtub.

"What changed?" she asked.

"I don't know. Maybe the fact that Mick isn't here to find out."

She choked out, "Do you regret it?"

Callum didn't hesitate. "No, not at all."

Gabriele was about to tell him she felt the same way when she startled at the clicking of the door handle. It squeaked as it opened and a large shadow filled the space.

RIDE ON A JET STREAM

Callum's eyes blinked rapidly in the sudden bright light. He glanced to the ceiling to find the source—a bare bulb hung off-center in the room. A man stood beneath it with the attached string still pressed between dark fingers. Callum recognized him from the intel MI5 had gathered. Bushy black brows arched over dark, deep-set eyes. His nose protruded over thin lips. Aban Vaziri.

Callum wondered where Agent Rebani was and if he was aware of Callum's predicament.

He could feel Gabriele's pulse in her wrist race as Aban Vaziri grew nearer. He didn't speak, but held out something in his hand. A bottle. Water.

"Can you untie us?" Callum said.

Aban Vaziri responded by shoving the bottle in his mouth. Callum opened wide and gulped the tepid water. Aban Vaziri moved to Gabriele's side and Callum could hear her taking long gulps.

Aban Vaziri didn't stay to chat. He tugged the string on the bulb, plunging them back into darkness. He used the light from his phone to guide himself out. Callum heard the click of the door lock when he left.

"They must need us to survive the night," Gabriele said.

"We might wish we hadn't."

It was a morbid thing to say, and Callum wished he could take the words back.

Her voice filled the small space once again. "Tell me about Iraq."

He wasn't surprised that she was asking him about that. It was something he hated to talk about, but since it looked like this was a night meant to cleanse the soul, he would make an exception.

"I was only there for eleven months before all British troops were pulled out. I don't have those horror stories some do of getting shot at or watching a mate die. Ironically, I hadn't been shot until I left the army and joined MI5.

"But I saw the effect of the war on the people. Civilians with missing limbs. Children without parents. Dead eyes, sunken from lack of water and nourishment. We tried to help the villages we passed through by handing out water and energy bars. Sometimes they cheered because we were there, and sometimes they booed and pretended to shoot with fingers folded in the shape of a gun."

Callum sighed. "Did we do any good by being there? I don't know."

He leaned his head back so Gabriele could rest hers against his. Touching, even in this very limited way, soothed him. He felt a connection to Gabriele Baumann that went beyond his brother. It wasn't something he could explain. It was just there, had been from the moment he'd met her if he was being honest. All the while he was trying to push her away, something else was calling her to him.

Callum's body sagged with exhaustion. What he wouldn't give to be able to lie down. He craved sleep. He drifted off into shallow unconsciousness. Somewhere in the murkiness, he thought he heard an angel sing.

> *Ride on a jet stream*
> *Fly like a kite on a string*
> *Drift on a daydream*
> *High like a bird on the wing,*
> *Where time doesn't mean a thing*
> *'cause you're lifting me high*
> *High above the wind and the rain*
> *When I need a place to go*
> *To free my soul*
> *You lift me up again*

Gabriele's voice filled the empty room, an ethereal essence lighting it with life and hope. Callum latched on to each word, soaking in the beauty of her voice, letting it caress and embrace him.

> *Sooner or Later*
> *I feel the weight of the world on my soul*
> *But your love is greater*
> *And like gravity, it never let's go*
> *Of me*
> *I can't lose for trying*
> *'cause you're lifting me high*
> *High above the wind and the rain*
> *But I need a place to go*
> *Lord, to free my soul*
> *Then you lift me up again*

HEART & SOUL

The silence that descended when she stopped singing blanketed the room with something thick and warm as if a presence had entered with Gabriele's voice. Callum's skin broke out in bumps.

He whispered, "That was beautiful."

She was beautiful. He wished he could see her face. He brought his memory of her to his mind's eye, hoping, praying he'd get to see it once again.

"Did you write that?" he asked.

"No," she said softly. "It's my sister's song. She went through a few dark years after her accident. Music is the Baumann family way of coping with deep pain."

Callum knew Gabriele was speaking from experience. "It's good that you have that," he said.

"We can't give up, Callum. There has to be a way out."

Callum glanced up to where the light bulb hung from the ceiling. "Maybe there is."

FLY LIKE A KITE ON A STRING

The door creaked open and the light snapped on. Aban Vaziri returned and this time he had company. Gabriele's heart seized. She'd seen the scruffy face of the new guy on the news. Yameen Jabour. He wielded power in Al Qaeda. Whatever he wanted with them couldn't be good.

He stood in between them so she and Callum could turn their heads and see him. His piercing dark gaze zeroed in on Callum's face. "Welcome, Mr. Jones."

Callum didn't return his greeting.

"I don't have a lot of time, so if you'd kindly give me the information I need, we can see to your release."

Gabriele felt Callum stiffen behind her, but he said nothing.

"What I need to know, Mr. Jones, is the flight details for our friend from Israel. We know he'll be traveling on a private jet. I need to know which airport, flight number and departure time."

Gabriele's breath hitched. The Prime Minister from Israel's meeting in London was to end tomorrow. His plane was their target.

"I don't know," Callum said with a low voice.

Yameen Jabour nodded to Aban Vaziri who stepped out of Gabriele's line of sight. A sickening crack rang out as Callum's head flicked back sharply. A groan.

"Callum!"

"Let's try this again, *Agent* Jones," Yameen Jabour said calmly.

This time Aban Vaziri produced a gun. He held it to Callum's temple and Gabriele whimpered.

"Still nothing?" Yameen Jabour asked. "So brave. How about this?" He nodded to Aban Vaziri who moved the barrel of the gun several centimetres and pressed it against Gabriele's head. She bit her lip and closed her eyes. Her pulse thundered loudly in her ears. Sweat broke out over her lip.

"Are you ready to say good-bye to your girlfriend? Or rather, should I say, your sister-in-law?"

Yameen Jabour had confirmed that they knew whom Gabriele was and that she hadn't been collateral damage in their capture of an MI5 agent.

Aban cocked the gun.

"Stop!" Callum said. "I'll talk. Just put the gun down."

Aban took his cue from Yameen and lowered his weapon to his side.

Callum sighed. He should resign himself to their deaths and not let the words escape his mouth. But he couldn't let her die.

"Flight 106, 16:00, Gatwick."

Yameen Jabour's full lips pulled up into a humourless smile. "I hope you are telling the truth, Mr. Jones. Otherwise, the outcome will not be good for Ms Baumann or yourself."

They left, plunging Gabriele and Callum into darkness.

"Are you okay?" Callum asked.

She let out a small, "Yes." She was better than Callum who suffered with a wounded shoulder and a blow to the face.

Her eyes had re-adjusted to the darkness, which was lit with only the moonlight from the window. They were in a cellar of some kind. In front of her was a row of empty shelves. She could see ring marks on the lower boards where jars of canned fruit and vegetables had once been stored.

"If we could break that light bulb somehow," Callum said in a whisper, "we could use the glass to cut the tape. Though I don't know how we can reach that."

Gabriele glanced up. "I don't think we can, but there's something else we can use." Callum faced away from the shelves so he couldn't see what she saw, a forgotten jar of fruit at the end of one of the lower shelves. It was pushed to the back and in the corner and easy to miss. She spotted it only because of her sitting position.

"There are shelves in front of me, Callum, and a jar. If we can reach it and break it…"

She felt him nod. "We have to move quietly. There might be someone nearby on the other side of that door."

It took a few tries before they found a rhythm, shuffling their two chairs awkwardly and slowly, back and forth, moving centimetres at a time. Gabriele broke into a sweat, and her head ached, and she could only imagine how hard it was for Callum. She at least hadn't been shot. It felt like eternity before they reached the shelves.

"I think I can knock it off with my feet," Gabriele said.

It took a huge effort to lift both of her feet to the shelf a half metre off the ground while tied to a chair. Her stomach muscles screamed as she worked to get a toe behind the jar. Its sugary juices had created an adhesive and the jar was stubbornly stuck. She kicked at it to loosen it. The jar toppled over. All she had to do now was push it over the edge.

It rolled and landed on the cement floor with a thick thwack. Gabriele froze. She listened intently for the sound of steps approaching from the other side of the door and breathed out in relief when none came. She lowered her feet to the ground and wished she could pat out the muscle cramp in her stomach.

The broken jar lay at her feet. The sweet scent of plums wafted up, and she breathed it in. Her stomach rolled in response. Too bad the fruit was ruined by splintered glass.

"Bad news, Callum. They're plums."

"As long as I don't eat any, I'm fine."

"How are we going to get the glass?"

"We have to tip ourselves over," Callum said. "But first we need to situate ourselves so our hands can reach it once we're down."

"That sounds unpleasant."

"I promise you it will be."

With every shuffle Gabriele's head felt like it would explode. She grit her teeth and willed herself to do what had to be done. They had turned until they were perpendicular to the jar.

"Ready?" Callum asked.

"Yes."

They began a rocking motion that catapulted them over to their sides. Gabriele's head smacked against the cement, and she couldn't help but cry out a little. Callum moaned. The cold from the cement leached through her blouse and she shivered.

Callum spoke, "We have to shift down a couple inches"

They worked the toppled chairs toward the shelves.

"Let me reach for the glass," Callum said. "I'll do the cutting."

Gabriele's head pounded, and she didn't have the strength to argue.

"I got a piece."

Gabriele felt the tape tighten as Callum twisted to work the glass shard back and forth. She winced when the glass nicked her hand but kept silent. Quite suddenly the tape loosened. Gabriele's heart leapt. It was working!

Callum pulled the tape off their hands and they worked rapidly stripping off the tape that bound their chests and their ankles. Callum picked up the chair with his good arm and carried it to the window. He hoisted himself up and fiddled with the lock. The window didn't budge.

"It's locked."

Gabriele felt a new wave of fear. If Aban Vaziri came back and found them like this, they'd be dead for sure.

Callum removed a shoe and put his fist in it. Then he punched the window, breaking the glass. He broke away as many of the jagged edges as he could with the sole of the shoe before reaching down and putting it back on.

He eased off the chair. "You first."

Gabriele climbed up. She counted on Callum to boost her so she wouldn't have to put her bare hands on the window edge.

HEART&SOUL

There was so much glass. There was no way she could get out unscathed, but there was no time to worry about that. She held back a yelp as her skin tore, but she made it through. She turned to help Callum. The window was so small, he could barely squeeze his shoulders through. His face twisted with the pain of pushing through the sharp edges of the hole. Gabriele took his good hand and pulled. Callum landed on the ground with a huff.

Gabriele grabbed his left hand, and they started running. They were in a rural area with a grassy meadow that extended for many kilometres. The house behind them was the only one she could see in the dim moonlight. Ahead was a forested area. If they could make it to the trees, they could hide.

They were almost there when she heard the first shot fire. Callum yelled out and collapsed beside her, pulling her down with him.

Gabriele grabbed at Callum's face. Was he breathing? Was he alive? "Callum!"

He groaned, and she whimpered with relief. "What happened?"

"My leg."

Gabriele could make out the dark stain growing on Callum's leg. She ripped off her blouse and quickly tied a tourniquet above the injury. Callum winced as she tightened it. "They're coming, Callum. We have to keep going!"

Gabriele helped Callum to his feet, propping herself under his arm as he limped towards the woods. Another shot was fired and Gabriele flinched.

"Go, Gabriele! I'm slowing you down."

"No! I'm not leaving you. Now shut up. We don't have time to argue."

They reached the trees as a third shot went off.

She yelled, "We have to find a place to hide."

The forest was thick and the overlapping branches created an umbrella that blocked out the moonlight. They stumbled over exposed roots and Callum grunted with an effort to keep from shouting out in pain.

They forged ahead blindly. Gabriele kept an arm stretched out, moving branches out of the way, making sure they didn't get clotheslined. Her skin burned as branches scraped against her exposed midriff. She didn't have time to think about the fact that she wore only a bra on top and had the weight of Callum's body pressed against her. They just had to keep ahead of their pursuers.

The ground gave way suddenly, and they tumbled down an incline. Their bodies twisted in the wet, leaf-lined forest floor. Gabriele held her breath, clinging to Callum. When they landed with a thud at the bottom, Gabriele couldn't breathe. Leaves fell on her head and she waved at them frantically.

Callum moaned. "Are you okay?"

Gabriele inhaled sharply. "Yeah. Just had the wind knocked out of me."

"I think we're in a hole."

Gabriele groped the darkness. Damp earth encircled them, beneath and on all sides. They must've landed in an abandoned fox lair.

She heard voices in the distance and quickly covered the opening of the hole above with fallen leaves and twigs. As long as the men didn't step directly on top of them they might escape detection.

She felt Callum's arm snake around her shoulders, pulling her close. She curled up against him, with her cheek on his chest. His breathing was shallow and labored. Her chest tightened with worry. He needed a doctor.

The voices grew louder. The wind had picked up and a rustle through the trees covered the sound of their breathing. She spotted a beam of light through the blanket of leaves. The men were close.

She held her breath.

One of the men spoke. "They have to be here somewhere."

The beam of light grew brighter, cutting the darkness with swift strokes.

Another voice responded. "He's injured. They couldn't have gone far."

The crunching of their footsteps grew dimmer as the men continued their search, farther on. Gabriele exhaled.

"We need to keep going." Callum's voice was labored and so quiet, Gabriele almost missed it. "I have to warn my team. Tell them about the new target."

"It's too dangerous," she said. "They're still out there, looking. They'd hear us. We have to wait."

But Gabriele agreed they couldn't wait long. She worried about Callum's injuries, especially his leg. "You need a doctor." She was afraid he might bleed out, but if they left now, they'd be discovered and dead for sure.

Callum's fingers ran along her face. "It's just a flesh wound. I'll live."

Gabriele snuggled in closer in an effort to keep warm and wrapped a leg over Callum's body. "Soon it will be dawn so we can at least see where we're going."

They were broken, hungry and cold, but they were alive. And exhausted. Gabriele couldn't remember ever being so tired.

HIGH LIKE A BIRD ON THE WING

She awoke to the raucous chirping of birds and a major kink in her neck. Callum mumbled something.

"Are you awake?" she asked, lifting herself up. She brushed away the leaves that rested on her and stood up carefully to peek out of the hole.

"Unfortunately." Callum groaned and pulled himself up into a sitting position. "I had hoped I'd just had an extremely vivid bad dream and would awake in the comfort of my own bed."

"How's your leg?"

"Excruciating."

Gabriele reached for his arm, helping him to a standing position. They stood facing each other waist deep in autumn foliage. Callum's face had darkened with more beard growth, though his skin had grown pale. Grey circles deepened under dark eyes that scrutinized her. They moved from her face, down her neck and landed on the bare skin of her cleavage.

Gabriele blushed and crossed her arms, feeling weirdly modest.

Callum blinked repeatedly. "Where's your blouse?"

"It's tied around your leg."

She scurried out of the hole and extended her hand. Callum accepted it and she hoisted him out.

"Damn, that hurts."

"You've been shot twice. I expect that it does hurt."

Gabriele had her own aches and pains. She rubbed the tender lump that remained on her head from the blow that knocked her out. Her skin was scratched from broken glass and sharp branches. Red lines crossed her belly and arms. Her palms felt shredded.

And she was cold. She wrapped her arms around herself and shivered. "We should find a road and wave down help."

Callum removed his shirt and Gabriele gaped. "What are you doing?"

He handed it to her. "It's a bloody mess, but it'll keep you warm."

"What about you?"

He grinned. "I guess *you'll* have to keep me warm."

She couldn't believe he was flirting at a time like this. She accepted the shirt though, despite its crusty, smelly condition.

Gabriele's throat scratched as she swallowed, feeling like it was going to close up if she didn't get something to drink soon. She plucked a leaf off a tree and tipped it into her mouth, letting the dew dribble in. It wasn't much, but it helped. She handed one to Callum and picked another for herself.

"You think it's okay to eat these?" she asked.

"The leaves?"

"Yeah. I'm not familiar with English forests. A lot can be poisonous."

Callum's eyes scoured the ground. "Look for clover."

He clearly meant the three-leaf variety and not Lennon's ex. Gabriele crouched low. "Here's some."

A batch grew at the base of a tree. She plucked a fist full for Callum, who accepted the offering with an outreached hand. Then she picked a few for herself and stuffed them in her mouth. It tasted like alfalfa grass.

"Do you think they're going to come looking for us again?" she asked.

Callum nodded. "We should get going. We have to get help. Find a phone. If we don't…"

He didn't have to finish. Gabriele knew. An assassination would take place that would greatly undermine the tenuous peace currently present in the Middle East. Possibly begin a war.

Gabriele tucked herself in under his arm. She felt completely comfortable there, she acknowledged. She couldn't deny her attraction to him. And not because of his resemblance to Lennon. He wasn't Lennon in any way but looks. He was forceful and focused. He had strong opinions and approached life with a fierce fearlessness she admired.

They could be good for each other.

It felt counterintuitive to head back in the direction of the farm house but that was also the way to the road, and they had to find it if they hoped to flag anyone down.

Except she couldn't tell if they were going in the right direction. The forest was a repeating pattern of trees and fallen leaves. The low cloud cover distributed the morning light, and it wasn't clear under the canopy of thick branches which way the sun was rising. And even if she could get her inner compass sorted, she didn't actually know where the farmhouse was since they'd escaped in the dark.

Gabriele's mind was foggy with sleep deprivation and her throat burned from thirst. She listened for road noises and thought she heard a lorry rumble in the distance. She turned Callum towards the noise.

She grunted under his weight. Her shoulders ached, and she strained her back and legs. Callum's breathing was quick and shallow, and his face was covered in a sweaty sheen. His knees buckled and he almost pulled her to the ground.

"Callum?" He was pale and the bandaging on his bare shoulder was blood soaked.

"I'm slowing us down," he said. "You need to go without me."

Anxiety lodged in her throat. She couldn't bear to leave him, but he was right. She could cover ground and get help much more quickly on her own. She helped him settle in against the trunk of a tree and gathered brush around him to conceal him.

She wished they had some water. She scoured the area and gathered up more clover. "Here. Eat these. I'll be back as fast as I can."

She kissed him on the lips, lingering for just a moment before running off.

Gabriele's feet caught in the debris of the autumn forest floor, snagging in loose branches and stumbling on uneven terrain. Her lungs heaved until she had to stop, bend at the hips and suck in air. She ran her tongue along dry lips and folded her arms around her stomach. She couldn't remember when she last ate. Spots swam in front of her eyes.

The faint grumble of intermittent vehicle engines motivated her to keep going. She was almost at the road. The whoosh of her own loud breaths filled her ears as she broke through the forest into the tall grass of the field. Gabriele could see the road. She sprinted with her last bit of energy and then cried out as her body slammed onto the ground. Her ankle screamed with pain. She'd been so focused on the roadway ahead, she didn't see the hole in the ground in front of her. She let out a groan as she lifted herself into a seated position to examine it. Already, the swelling was severe.

Gabriele hopped onto her good leg and yelped when she tried to put weight on her injured foot. She hopped two steps before falling. Tears ran down her face. The pain was extreme but the thought that she was this close to the road but too far to flag for help was intolerable. She shifted her weight to her forearms and dragged herself through the grass, wincing with every drag of her bad ankle.

The hard stalks of dry grass bit her flesh, but she forged on, nearing the ditch. She heard a car approach. If she could just get to the curb before it passed by.

Then it stopped.

A car wouldn't stop without first being flagged down on this stretch of road unless it was driven by someone looking for something.

She ducked into the grass, hoping it concealed her.

Gabriele's heart thudded in her ears. If they spotted her...

She kept still, making herself as flat as she could. She had to let them look for Callum if she hoped at all to escape their notice and find help.

She could only pray they wouldn't find him first.

A voice called out. "Callum?"

Gabriele closed her eyes. *Please don't see me.*

"Agent Jones, it's me, Rebani."

Rebani. Gabriele overheard something about an agent working on the inside of the terrorist cell. That was what they called him. Wasn't it?

Wasn't it?

If she revealed her position, and he wasn't on their side, she and Callum were dead.

Rebani started toward the forest, his back away from her. He held a phone to his ear and his voice carried. "I don't see him. No, he's not with the cell. I'm here without their knowledge. No sign of Gabriele Baumann yet, either. I was informed this morning that Agent Jones had been shot. I'm requesting a medic."

Gabriele blinked hard. Rebani was talking to the grid.

"Agent Rebani!" she called, "Over here!"

Rebani swiveled, and his eyes widened. "I found Ms Baumann. I'll call you back."

Agent Rebani approached. He had short black hair, brown skin and a determined look in his dark eyes.

"Gabriele Baumann?"

"Yes."

"Are you injured?"

"My ankle. I twisted it."

"Where is Agent Jones? Is he okay?"

"He's alive." At least she hoped he still was. "I had to leave him in the forest to get help." She gave him directions as best she could.

"Oh, there's something you need to know," she said, holding Rebani's gaze. "The Israeli jet is a target today."

"Today?"

"Yes, the Prime Minister flies out on a private jet at 16:00, right?"

Rebani nodded slowly.

"Jabour knows."

"I'm going to ring headquarters. Will you be all right if I leave you? Help is on its way."

She nodded. "Yes. Go."

DRIFT ON A DAYDREAM

Callum's eyes snapped open. He took in his foreign surroundings: the dimly light florescent lighting, the white curtain pulled around his bed, the IV pole with a line running to the vein that bulged on the inside of his elbow.

Memories from the last twenty-four hours flooded his mind. He and Gabriele had been chased, captured and tied up. He'd been shot. Twice.

Gabriele. The fear etched on her face.

A gun pointed at her head.

He closed his eyes as his body felt the echo of his terror. *He could've lost her.*

And he'd sent her off on her own to fetch help. A million horrible things could've gone wrong. He hated that he'd put her in so much danger and vowed never to do it again.

A middle-aged nurse with flushed cheeks came with breakfast. She laid the tray on the table and swung it over the bed. Callum pushed a button that raised the back of the bed until he was in a sitting position.

He thanked her and asked, "How is Gabriele Baumann? The girl who came in with me yesterday?"

"She's fine." She grabbed his wrist to take his pulse. "Better than you. I suspect she'll be released sometime later today."

Callum smiled at her, relieved to hear the news.

Paula was the first to visit him, not long after he'd eaten. She pulled up a chair next to the IV stand and sat straight-backed. She wore her standard blue suit, and her hair was tied back in a simple ponytail.

"You look well, considering," she said.

"Thanks," Callum muttered.

He'd briefed her on the events the evening before, but she came with more clarifying questions, which he answered to the best of his ability. Then she surprised him with a comment and a question about Gabriele.

"Normally, we'd approach her ourselves," she continued, "but in light of your... relationship with her, we thought we'd give you a chance to submit an opinion."

His back stiffened. "No, I don't like it. I don't agree. My vote is no."

Paula jerked at the force of his words. "I see. Well, then, we'll table the idea." She pushed the chair back and, to Callum's relief, changed the subject. "How are you feeling?"

Like *Scheisse*, as Gabriele would say. He had a hole in his shoulder and a chunk of flesh missing from his thigh where the last bullet had clipped him. He'd arrived dehydrated with moderate hypothermia, which the IV and warm blankets had taken care of thankfully.

"I'm fine. A little sore, but the painkillers are working. I had breakfast and kept it down. I'm on the mend."

"Good." Paula stood to leave. "Take as much time as needed to recover. Ring me when you think you're ready to come back to work." She paused at the door. "You *are* coming back?"

Callum grunted. "Yes."

The door swung shut behind Paula, and a moment later there was another knock. Gabriele poked in her head. "Are you up for a visitor?"

Her green eyes latched onto his. She looked freshly showered and wore clothes he hadn't seen before. Her face was scratched and bruised, and he noted the thin, red marks on her arms and hands.

His heart flipped at the sight of her. She was something he wanted but couldn't have. A beautiful torment.

"Come in," he said.

Gabriele pulled up the chair that had recently been vacated by Paula to the side of his bed. She stared at him with an intensity that unnerved him. The way she felt about him was written all over her face, and he hated what he was about to do.

"You look... better," she said.

"Doc says another couple days on my back here, then I should be good to go."

"Back to work?"

"Eventually."

She took his hand and pressed it to her face, and he almost

lost his resolve. Her skin was so soft, and she smelled like dew. Her dark hair fell over her eyes, and she pushed it behind her ears. She swallowed like she was trying to gain the courage to say something that frightened her.

"Callum, I'm so glad you are okay. Yesterday, after the van had run us off the road and that man held you at gunpoint, I was terrified that I was about to watch you die. Everything happened so fast, but in that moment, in that millisecond, I knew I…"

Callum's chest tightened with dread. *Please don't say it. Please don't say it.*

Their eyes locked and Gabriele whispered, *"Ich liebe dich."*

The oxygen whisked out of the room. Gabriele's eyelids fluttered, growing glassy with her declaration. She squeezed his hand, waiting for him to respond.

He inhaled deeply and forced himself to tear his eyes away from her. "You're just caught up in the moment, Gabriele. We've lived through a very emotional crisis. Of course it will make us feel bonded." He glanced back at her. "But that doesn't mean you love me."

Her face fell, and she flushed red with embarrassment as if Callum had just slapped her. He felt like an ass.

She clasped her hands on her lap. "I think I know my own mind, Mr. Leatherby or Mr. Jones or Mr. whoever-the-hell-you-think-you-are. If you really want me to leave England, I'll leave. Just say it."

Callum applied a blank, emotionless expression. He pushed against the desire threatening to take over his will. He almost reached for her, almost pulled her to his chest so he could breath in her hair. So he could kiss her deeply.

Instead, he forced himself to do something he knew he'd

hate himself for forever. He stared at her and said, "I want you to leave."

HE CAME FROM A SEASIDE TOWN

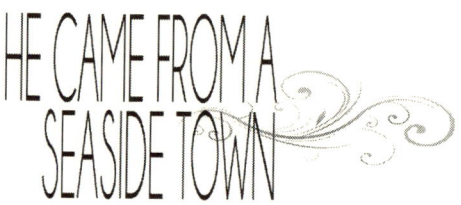

Gabriele felt like such an idiot—duped twice by two brothers! She really thought Callum had shared the feelings she'd developed for him. The way he'd looked at her. Stroked her hair. Kissed her lips.

Had it all been a put on?

She ground her back teeth to subdue the anger that burned in her chest. She took the bar rag and cleaned the tables in Callahan's Irish Pub. After Callum's heartless dismissal, Gabriele had decided she would sell the cottage and go back to Dresden. She'd had enough of the Leatherby family and couldn't wait to distance herself from them.

But once she returned to Emsworth, she found she wasn't so eager to go. The seascape soothed her nerves, and the truth was, she didn't relish the idea of moving back in with her parents. She needed her independence, and the fastest way to obtain that was to sell the cottage. A quick trip to a nearby realty office got the ball rolling, and within a couple of days, a For Sale sign was hung on both the street side and ocean side of the little house. Gabriele decided it would be worth staying until it sold, that way she could make sure it was clean and presentable. Leaving it locked up and empty wasn't a good idea.

Except that it didn't sell. Her realtor told her it was a bad time of year for selling seaside properties, but she was certain it would get snapped up in the spring.

Which meant she would stay until spring. Which meant she needed a job. Fortunately, her EU passport allowed her to work in England and equally fortuitous was the sudden opening at Callahan's when one of their waitresses quit suddenly, running off to Spain to elope with a guy she'd met on the internet.

Gabriele had been working at Callahan's for two of the five weeks she'd been back in Emsworth. She was grateful for the work and for the distraction. Ciara was becoming a friend, and Riley Callahan was a great boss.

The days were manageable with hardly a tear shed. It was a different story in the evenings when she returned to her empty cottage alone. The nights were long and lonely and she'd gone through more than her fair share of tissue boxes. Every morning and every night she'd look over at the house next door and wonder if Callum had come back. The darkened house was a daily disappointment, and she finally kicked herself in the butt and told herself in no uncertain terms to *get over him!*

"You're going to rub a hole straight through that table."

Ciara's voice pulled Gabriele out of her miry thoughts. "Oh, yeah."

"Is everything all right? You were somewhere else."

Gabriele glanced at Ciara. Her red hair was tied back in its usual messy knot. Her eyes were friendly, but she squinted with concern. Gabriele would've loved to tell Ciara everything. It would feel great to unburden herself.

But everything about Lennon and Callum was secret or classified and her personal involvement with both brothers was embarrassing. She forced a smile and shook her head. "I'm fine. Just daydreaming." She turned to Ciara, wanting to change the subject. "Are you going home for Christmas?"

"Ey. Christmas is a big deal for the Callahan clan. I couldn't opt out if I wanted to. You?"

"Yes. For a few days." Christmas was a special celebration for her family as well, and she wouldn't want to miss it. Last year had been deeply painful, being the first one since Lennon passed away, and this one would prove to be tough as well, but not as tough. Gabriele hoped each one would continue to get easier. She did miss her family, and she loved the German traditions surrounding the holiday.

"Ireland looks like such a beautiful place," Gabriele said. "I've always wanted to go there."

"Ah, you should go," Ciara said with a sparkle in her eye. "It is a wonderful place."

Gabriele straightened the condiment tray. "Then why'd you leave?"

Ciara paused and darted her eyes away from Gabriele. Gabriele could sense there was a story coming and waited.

"There was a lad I fancied. We were together for four years, and I really loved him. I believed he loved me. On the night I thought he was going to propose, he broke up with me instead. Turns out he'd found himself another girl in the next village and apparently I was the last to know. I was crushed and humiliated. It hurt too much to be there. So I left."

"I'm sorry to hear that," Gabriele said kindly. "If it's any consolation. I know exactly how you feel."

Sorrow flashed behind Ciara's eyes. "Is there a girl left on the earth that isn't nursing a broken heart?"

Gabriele pouted, then smiled, hoping to lighten the mood. The bell rang and Clover Swift entered with her on-again boyfriend Rupert. Gabriele took a deep breath. It was her job to take their orders. She returned to the bar to replace the cloth in the sink and grabbed her order pad. Riley was there, removing the tray from the cash register. He'd heard the bell as well and had paused in the middle of what he was doing to watch Clover and Rupert get seated. His gaze remained fixed on the blond until he realized that Gabriele was standing beside him, waiting to get through the narrow space.

"Oh, sorry," he said, looking like he got caught doing something he didn't want anyone to know he was doing.

Like pining for another guy's girlfriend?

He moved to the end of the bar, but he couldn't keep his eyes from darting to the table across the room.

Ciara returned with a tray of clean glasses.

"Does your brother fancy her?" Gabriele asked, gesturing between Riley and Clover.

Clover lowered her voice. "Another sad tale of unrequited love. My poor brother has had a thing for Clover Swift since he first moved to town. She's always been involved with one bloke or another and never seems to notice Riley. It doesn't help that he clams up and hides whenever she's around. His nerves get the best of him, poor lad." She arched a brow in warning. "You never heard it from me."

Gabriele grinned and patted her arm. "My lips are sealed."

Enough time had passed for Clover and Rupert to finish reviewing the menu. Gabriele straightened her shoulders, took a deep breath and walked to Clover's table. "Hi. Are you ready to order?"

Thankfully, they knew what they wanted, meat pie for him and a bowl of clam chowder for her, and Gabriele didn't have to spend any more time at the table than necessary. She delivered the order to the kitchen.

"Seems to me my brother's not the only one with a Clover Swift fascination," Ciara said. Gabriele jumped, embarrassed that she'd been caught staring. "Oh, well." She couldn't stop her curiosity. Her mind pictured Clover and Lennon together, the way they likely would've been if all this craziness hadn't happened. "She's pretty," she said lamely.

"And she dated Callum Leatherby's brother."

Gabriele flashed Ciara a startled look. Did she know about Lennon? How could she?

"What?" Ciara said with a smirk.

"Why would you say that? I mean, why do you think I would I care about that?"

"No reason. Just that the Leatherby brothers were the first thing we talked about, if you remember. And I thought there was something going on between you and Callum Leatherby. He was certainly your shadow for a while there."

Gabriele lowered her chin, feeling sheepish. "No, that was nothing. I haven't seen him for weeks."

The bell rang and Ciara's eyebrow arched as she glanced toward the door. "Well, speak of the devil."

I GAVE HIM EVERYTHING I HAD

Gabriele gripped the counter to steady herself. Callum Leatherby had come back to Emsworth. He was there, in the flesh, his dark eyes boring into her as he approached.

He wore his blue winter coat. His hair was a little longer than she remembered and his face freshly shaved.

She turned away, pretending to busy herself with items on the back wall. She straightened beer mugs and wine glasses, checked the drawer for... whatever. Her eyes pinched with tears, and her heart stammered out of control. She had to get ahold of her nerves. She didn't want him to see her fall apart or worse, think that he had anything to do with it. All this time she'd hoped to catch of glimpse of him in his house next door, and now with him standing only metres away, she wished she was anywhere in the world but here.

"Gabriele?"

Gabriele took a breath, then turned with eyes wide and feigned a calmness she didn't feel.

"Oh, hi. Can I get you something?"

Callum's eyes flickered with uncertainty. She wasn't sure what he expected from her? A big hug and a happy welcome home?

"A beer."

"Large or small?"

He slid onto a bar stool. "Large."

Gabriele grabbed a clean mug from the shelves behind her and held it under the tap. She kept her eye on the glass, tilting it carefully to monitor the foam level. The Brits, at least in these parts, didn't like a tall foam like the Germans did. She placed the full mug on a paper coaster and slid it over to Callum.

She didn't stay to chat. The order for Clover's table was up so she delivered it. She felt Callum's eyes on her back, and she worked to keep her hands still. The last thing she needed to do was dump the tray of food on the floor.

She returned the tray to the kitchen and then helped Riley set up the stage for open mic night, which was scheduled to start in less than an hour.

Gabriele hoped that Callum would be gone by the time she returned to the bar, but he remained seated, his beer only half gone.

He waved her over, and she reluctantly went to him. He was a paying customer after all.

"I need to talk to you. Can you take a break?"

She was due for a break soon, but she didn't know if she wanted to spend it with Callum. He was like a seam ripper. His mere presence was enough to pull her fragile emotional threads apart.

Gabriele's curiosity was stronger than her sense of self-preservation apparently because she found herself nodding. She had to know what Callum had to say for himself.

She left him to speak quickly to Ciara, informing her that she was taking her fifteen-minute break now, then led Callum to one of the empty booths.

Gabriele sank into the soft seat and covered her mouth with her hand. She wished she could cover her entire face, hide her eyes and the conflicting emotions that flashed behind them. She loved Callum and hated him in equal portions. She didn't want him to know about either struggle.

She placed her hands in her lap and stared boldly into his beautiful, mesmerizing dark eyes. "What do you want?"

He cracked a smile. "To see you."

She placed her hand on the table, shifting her weight to stand. "Fine. You saw me."

Callum reached for her wrist, his warm skin sending sparks up her arm and through her body. "Gabriele, please. Give me a moment."

She pulled her hand back sharply and lowered herself into her seat. She narrowed her eyes. "What game are you playing, Callum?"

He sighed. "No game. I really came to see you. I have something to tell you."

Gabriele folded her arms over her fluttering chest in an attempt to calm the raging war of emotions going on in her heart. She hated that Callum was here.

She loved that Callum was here.

"How are you, Gabriele? Really?"

She plastered on a phony smile. "I'm *great*."

His smile faltered at her forced exuberance. "Good," he said. "I'm glad."

"What did you want to tell me, Callum? What was so important that you had to come *all the way* to Emsworth?"

Callum leaned back and watched her. She squirmed under his scrutiny.

"I have a confession."

Gabriele gulped. Did this have to do with her declaration? The stupid little words she uttered to him in the hospital? *Ich liebe dich*. German for *I love you*.

"Okay?" Gabriele encouraged him to continue.

"The team wanted to recruit you. They were impressed with how you handled everything that happened to us. You kept your head, had good instincts, functioned under pressure even in the face of death. Hiring non-nationals isn't something the secret service normally does, so it speaks volumes that they're willing to waive protocol to have you.

"Gabriele, you saved my life, more than once. Plus, your language skills are an asset." He paused, then added, "I vetoed the decision."

Gabriele shook her head, stupefied.

"You're here to *recruit* me?"

"That and... well, yes. I'm still not in favour of it, but I concede that it was wrong of me to make that decision for you."

"You could've called and saved yourself a trip."

Callum held her gaze. "I wanted to see you."

Gabriele couldn't breathe. She still loved him. No matter how tough she thought she was, his brown eyes melted her. She glanced away.

"I'm not interested."

HEART&SOUL

Truth was, she'd love to take the job. Any other job would bore her to tears. She knew that about herself now. But she couldn't go to London to simply be Callum's colleague.

Something flashed behind Callum's eyes. Disappointment? Relief? He chugged back the rest of his beer before saying, "I'll pass that on."

WHY SHOULD I LOVE YOU?

"Are we finished?" Gabriele asked. "My break is over."

She hoped he'd nod and leave, but instead he said, "I'll have a platter of fish and chips, please."

Her eyes widened. He was ordering? He actually expected her to *serve* him? She had no choice. This was her job and he was a customer. She scowled. "Coming right up."

She delivered Callum's order to the kitchen and then waited on customers who'd filled the stools along the bar.

The first act began, a middle-aged woman with short spiky hair dyed a brilliant red. Gabriele forced her attention to stay on the woman.

"Man, you should see your face." It was Riley's voice. "Who got your knickers in a knot? Someone you want me to kick out?"

Riley looked at her with serious grey eyes, and Gabriele softened her expression. "I'm fine. Just wondering, do you think

HEART & SOUL

I could play tonight?"

"Sure. The list isn't full. When do you want to go on?"

"Next?"

The girl finished, and Riley jumped on the stage. "Wasn't she great? Give it up for Thelma!" He encouraged the crowd to applaud enthusiastically. "And next we have, Gabriele Baumann!"

Gabriele smirked when she saw Callum's eyebrows shoot up. She really hoped he liked the song she was about to sing.

She strapped on the house guitar and checked the tuning. Then she began.

He came from a seaside town,
Breakfast café with a worn-out lounge
Will he be remembered for things
I don't know

I gave him everything I had
Ran to his side every chance I got
Will I find true love again?
I hope so.

Heaven knows it,
I didn't see it 'til it was too late
Can I survive this?
I hope so.

He'll tell you anything you want,
Patch up your soul with his makeshift love
I swore I'd never see him again.
I did, though.

I don't know where to go,
I've never been here before
I can't make up my mind

Lee Strauss

I put on a smile

Heaven knows it,
I didn't see it 'til it was too late
Can I survive this?
I hope so.

And why should I love you?
I have no reasons as of right now
I guess it's time to move on

The crowd applauded and she thanked them. Callum clapped slowly and she felt him watch her as she made her way to the kitchen. She returned to him with his meal in hand.

"Nice song," he said as she lowered the plate to the table and pushed it in front of him. "Is it about Lennon or me?"

"Both. It starts off about Lennon. You kick in about halfway."

Callum grinned crookedly. "I'm honored. I've never had a song written about me before."

Fury flushed through Gabriele's chest. This was all just a big joke to him! She swiveled and stormed away. In seconds, she felt his hand on her arm.

"Gabriele?"

Her eyes moved from his hand on her arm to his face, and she shot him a withering look. "What?"

He released his hold. "I know you're mad, and I don't blame you. But I need to tell you one more thing. I moved Mick's body."

CAN I SURVIVE THIS?

Gabriele's mind raced to compute the words that had come from Callum's mouth. Anger flickered in her gut.

"You moved my husband's body? Without telling me?"

"I'm sorry, Gabi. I should've told you. I know that now. At the time it was a case of what you don't know won't hurt you. I needed him to be here, buried beside my parents. I hope you understand."

She sighed. Callum and his parents had more of a right to Lennon's body than she did. "How did you manage it?" A bizarre image of Callum sneaking into the graveyard in Dresden, dressed in black with a shovel in his hand, crossed her mind. "It's not like you're allowed to do that without notifying the next of kin. Which is me, by the way."

"The agency took care of those matters."

Gabriele huffed and crossed her arms. "Any other secrets you need to get off your chest?"

Callum's eyes flashed with sadness and he shook his head. "No. You know everything now. But I was wondering, would you like to go to the cemetrey with me?"

Gabriele couldn't say no to Callum's request. She'd been with Lennon for over a year and his wife for a month. She should know where his actual body lay. She wanted to know.

Callum waited for her until her shift ended and they huddled against the cold in the moonless night. Like everything in Emsworth, the cemetrey was in walking distance. It'd begun to snow and soon everything was covered in a blanket of white. The low lying clouds and windless evening deadened the sound. She heard her heart pulse in her ears.

They covered the distance in silence and Gabriele was thankful. She didn't think she had anything left to say to Callum. He led her through an impressive wrought iron gate behind a short hedge planted along a brick berm. They tread reverently between rows of concrete headstones. Eventually, Callum stopped in front of a cluster of gravestones and bent down to brush the snow off three stones belonging to Joseph Leatherby, Marla Leatherby, and a new darker stone that read *Mick Leatherby*. Gabriele crouched low and ran a finger over his name.

Callum bent down beside her. Their hot breaths clashed in the cool air in a white ghostly embrace.

"I loved him," he said quietly.

"I know you did," she answered softly. "I did, too."

Callum studied her. "I loved him. You were *in* love with him."

She held his gaze. "There are many different kinds of love."

His attention returned to the stone. "Thanks for coming."

She stepped away. Her blood pulsed madly as she stared at him and she couldn't stop from blurting, "Why didn't you want me?"

Callum stood and faced her, his dark eyes locking with hers. "I *do* want you. I don't want you to work for the MI5. It's dangerous as you well know. I almost lost you and I couldn't stand the thought of that ever happening again."

Callum stepped closer until they were almost touching. She stood still as he ran his finger under her chin causing her to quiver. "I want you." He leaned in, closing the distance between them. She held her breath. His lips brushed against hers.

Gabriele squeezed her eyes shut and whimpered. She knew these lips. She *loved* these lips. She was too weak to resist. She wrapped her arms around his neck and deepened the kiss, consuming him. She tilted her head back as his mouth moved along her jaw line to the base of her neck, and she let out a soft moan. She dreamed of this moment, longed for it. The last time they had kissed each other like this they were lying awkwardly in his dry bathtub. She'd wanted to devour him then. But that hadn't been love. It was lust.

Something had changed for her since. She loved him now. Was *in* love with him. But he... he was playing with her again. He was a heartless *player*.

She gripped his shoulders and pushed him away with a forceful shove. "Get away from me!"

His dark eyes flickered with confusion. "Gabi?"

"I'm not your plaything. And you're not mine. It's not what I want. It's not how I want it."

She stomped through the snow towards the gate. She couldn't get away from Callum fast enough.

"Gabriele!"

She felt his hand grip her arm, pulling her to a stop.

"I haven't been playing fair. I know that." He positioned himself in front of her, forcing her to look at him. "I might not know a load of German, but I do know what *Ich liebe dich* means. Gabi, I love you, too."

Gabriele looked to the sky. Her heart was a pummeled mess. She'd spent so much effort this last month trying to get over Callum. She'd convinced herself that she was better off without him. The Leatherby brothers had wrecked her.

An empty plastic bag tumbled across the cemetrey grounds in the cool wind. That was how Gabriele felt. Hollow. Aimless. Lost.

Her eyes burned with remorse and she wiped away a tear. "I don't believe you."

Callum swallowed hard, looking crushed. "I'm sorry I hurt you."

He wrapped her in his strong arms, pulling her tight to his chest. She bit her lip, remaining limp, and fought against an avalanche of tears just waiting to be unleashed. She wouldn't cry in front him.

Her throat was tight and dry, but she managed to say, "I have to go."

She forced herself to walk away.

He shouted out after her. "I'm leaving for London tomorrow at noon. Will you come with me?"

Gabriele hoped her refusal to look at him was answer enough.

I HOPE SO

Callum looked out of the upper-story window of his house toward the cottage. From this vantage point, he could see the back door leading to the sea. The terrace was empty, but the lights inside were on. Gabriele was up and awake.

And ignoring his texts.

He hoped she'd respond, hoped that she'd change her mind and tell him she'd come to London with him, but she had been pretty adamant when she left him in the cemetrey the previous night.

He scrolled through his messages to Gabriele. He'd started writing them a minute after she'd walked away.

Callum Jones
I know you don't believe me, but it's true. I love you.

Lee Strauss

I'm IN love with you.

Not because you were married to my brother.

It has nothing to do with him.

Except that he's the reason we met. I'm heartbroken he had to die, but if I get you, then something good came of it.

I want you.

Not as a plaything.

Though playing is fun, too. You have to admit. Right?

Did I mention I WANT you.

Not just for now.

Forever.

No one else.

You've ruined me for anyone else.

Come work with me.

We can conquer evil together – bwahaha

Gabriele?

I LOVE YOU

> That was last night
> He began again this morning while eating breakfast.

Callum Jones
Guess what I'm drinking? Coffee with foamed milk. I love it because it

reminds me of you. The sexy little foamed milk mustache you get when you take that first sip. The way you run your fingers around your mouth to wipe it off. Makes me crazy.

I'm crazy about you.

CRAZY

He'd tried ringing, but she didn't answer.

Callum Jones
Gabi, you've never seen my flat in London. I bet you'd like it. Nice view of the Thames.

Funny thing. There's a coffee foamer in the cupboard. I have NO idea how that got there.

HOPE did it, I think.

I hope you'll come with me.

I hope you'll believe me.

I love you.

He checked the time on his phone: 11:30. He wiped down the kitchen, and then went upstairs to clean his teeth and pack his bags. He took another look out the window to the cottage, this time from the room that had a view to the back street. He didn't know what he thought he'd see. Gabriele packed up and waiting at the curb would be a nice sight but apparently, it was a fantasy, because she was nowhere to be seen.

Callum returned to the main level, double checked the locks on the window and doors and set the security alarm.

It was almost noon. He'd promised to be back at the grid by two, and if he wanted to stop by his flat first he had to leave soon. He checked his texts once more. Nothing. He almost rang her, but her silence told him everything already. Disappointment smacked him hard. He had to accept that she wasn't coming.

Callum Jones
You've made your decision. I don't like it, but I respect it.

Ich liebe dich.

Callum tossed his bag into the backseat of his refurbished Smart Car and hopped in. He pushed the garage door opener, slid the car into gear and drove away.

Just as he turned the corner onto High Street, his phone buzzed. He pulled it out of his pocket so fast he almost dropped it. His mouth widened into a deep grin as he read the text.

Gabriele Baumann
I believe you.

Callum slowed, pulled a tight U-y, and raced back to the cottage. She stood at the end of her walkway. He skidded to a stop and leaped out. He wrapped his arms around her tightly and breathed in her scent, imagining everything he almost lost. He cupped her face with his hands and stared into her gorgeous green eyes.

His lips found hers, and she kissed him hard like she meant it. Like she loved him. Like she really did believe him.

BUTTERFLY KISSES

It was a beautiful spring day with a bright blue sky and dazzling sunshine. A day as spectacular as this one couldn't be wasted, especially since it was a rare day off from work. Gabriele held Callum's hand as they walked across the pedestrian bridge perpendicular to St. Paul's Cathedral to the south side of the Thames. They stopped to watch the tugboats scoot beneath them and to take in the iconic Tower Bridge to the east.

Gabriele worked as a translator and interpreter for MI5. Much of her work was done at the grid behind a desk in front of a computer, but more often lately she was in the field, which she loved. Callum didn't like it when she left the safety of the office, but he agreed to not impede her in any way. If it was going to work between them, they had to respect each other, including professionally. They both knew the risks, that one or both of them might not live through the day.

It made their relationship even more precious.

Callum turned to her. "Do you think about him often?"

She knew he meant Lennon. And it would be a lie if she said no.

"Yes. Do you?"

"Yes."

Lennon would always have a place in their hearts, but he no longer came between them.

"I wonder if he sees us," Gabriele said. "If he knows."

Callum shrugged. "I don't know. But I knew my brother, and he'd want me to take care of you." He leaned in and kissed her gently.

They continued until they reached the opposite bank and turned west in the direction of the London Eye. The path along the Thames was a popular one for joggers, tourists and families.

They stopped at an ice-cream truck and ordered cones. Ahead Gabriele spotted a busker playing a guitar.

"Let's watch her," she said.

They stood amongst the gathering crowd and took in the talented woman's performance. She was petite, and she wore a long flowing, shimmery skirt that reached the tops of her black army boots. A baggy, grey cardigan hung loosely over her shoulders. Her head appeared to be bald, covered with a colourful satin scarf.

She was a good musician with a clear, high-pitched folksy voice.

Gabriele felt her phone buzz in her pocket and reached for it with her free hand. She smiled when she saw her friend's name.

Julia Milch
How's London treating you? Still like your secretarial job?

HEART&SOUL

Gabriele tossed the last bit of her cone into a trash bin, then responded.

Gabriele Baumann
The city's great fun. The job's a bit of a bore, but the people are interesting.

Julia Milch
And Callum? He's still playing nice?

Gabriele shot a wry smile Callum's way.

Gabriele Baumann
Oh, yeah.

Julia Milch
He better be. Oh, Ulrich's here. I think he wants to marry me. More later!

Gabriele chuckled. She wouldn't be surprised. Julia was a catch for any man who could keep up with her.

Gabriele Baumann
Keep me posted!

"Who was that?" Callum asked.

"Julia. Just checking in." Julia knew that Callum was Lennon's twin, but she didn't know about the grid. She still believed that Callum worked for the city's sustainability department. It's what everyone in Dresden believed.

A few listeners threw coins into the girl's empty guitar case when she finished the song. Gabriele approached and dropped a bill inside.

"Thanks," the girl said. She looked pale with bluish circles under her eyes. Her eyebrows were barely there.

There was a small pile of CDs on the ground near the case. Gabriele picked one up. *Anna* was embossed on the top. "I'll take them all, Anna."

The girl's invisible eyebrows jumped in surprise. "Really?"

"Yeah, I have a lot of birthdays coming up." Not exactly true, but there was something about Anna—her vulnerability, her physical weakness—that made Gabriele want to help. Plus, she knew how hard it was to play for strangers. To put yourself out there like that. It took guts.

"Thank you," Anna said with feeling. "You don't know how grateful I am."

"It's my pleasure."

Gabriele returned to Callum's side and threaded her fingers through his hand. She perked up as Anna began to play a cover.

Gabriele smiled. "That's my sister's song."

"Ah, 'Flesh and Bone,'" Callum said. "I thought it was a Hollow Fellows' song?"

Gabriele grinned. Sebastian's band had made headway into the British music scene recently.

"It is," she agreed. "Eve cowrote it with Sebastian Weiss."

"Cool." Callum draped an arm around her shoulder and squeezed. "I'm only two degrees of separation from someone famous."

She laughed. "I'm only one."

He poked her playfully. "Have you written anything new?"

"Not recently. Too busy stopping people from blowing up the city."

"Well, you know what they say about all work and no play."

She stared up at him. "Makes Gabi a dull girl?"

HEART & SOUL

He lifted her chin and gazed steadily in her eyes. He leaned in and whispered breathily into her ear. "There is absolutely nothing dull about you."

He kissed her with soft butterfly kisses as Anna played in the background, *"All I wanna do is find love...."*

Please enjoy this sample from

Peace & Goodwill

(A Christmas Novella)
by Lee Strauss

A Time and a Season
Belle

Belle Vaughn swallowed the gluey lump that formed in her throat as she arranged the winter scene in the window of King's Books used bookstore. Mrs. Cowen could be very particular, and she wanted the miniature replicas of the popular landmarks of London and all its miniature inhabitants "to delight and entice" prospective shoppers into the shop.

Belle arranged the little carolers around the mini version of Saint Paul's Cathedral. Trees and park benches dotted the edges of a curvy blue ribbon that represented the River Thames. Small bridges, including the famed Tower Bridge, crossed the river. There were even tiny lamp posts and street cars, including the iconic red double-decker buses. She sprinkled shiny, white confetti over everything for a snow-like touch and plugged in the string of white lights she'd tacked around the window earlier that day.

She gasped at little at her creation, a beautiful, perfect, little world, and the pang in her heart deepened. A glance through the window reminded her that the real world wasn't so magical. She didn't live in the romantic ideal of London central but in the lesser-visited eastern end which was crowded with the poor and working poor like herself.

Outside, holiday shoppers scampered hunched over, chins buried into scarves, bodies pressed into the wind, with no time or inclination to stop and gaze at the fanciful window display Belle had created. The real streets beyond the glass were dirty and the sky was a brooding grey. Nasty weather systems were attacked the United Kingdom from the arctic regions of the pacific.

Belle sighed and returned to the counter where a stack of books waited for her to catalogue, price and shelve.

"Any plans for Christmas this year, love?" Mrs. Cowen asked. She asked Belle this every year and every year Belle shook her head sheepishly. No. She was an orphan and without family. She lived alone in her little flat for the last three years since her mother had passed away, and didn't even have a pet because her miserable landlord forbade it.

"You're welcome to spend it with us," Mrs. Cowen said with a small smile. "Again."

Again. Mrs. Cowen was being polite, but the truth was that Belle's presence at Mrs. Cowen's family Christmas was an intrusion. For the last two years, she was the only non-family member sitting around the Cowen's dinner table. Everyone was always pleasant and polite—how could they not be? Belle was to be pitied. No parents, no family. It was their *duty* to include her. If the dinners were uncomfortable, her arrival to the Christmas morning gift opening was downright painful. After Mrs. Cowen's daughter and two granddaughters greeted her with fake smiles and stiff hugs, they basically pretended she wasn't in the room.

Being alone was preferable to being invisible.

Mrs. Cowen wore billowing blouses and skirts that hung loosely on her tall, thin frame. Her greying, blond hair was permed into tight, short curls and she penciled in her eyebrows, thin stark lines above sagging eyelids too tired to resist gravity any longer. Belle put on her brave face and stared at her employer. "Thank you so much for the invitation, Mrs. Cowen, but I've accepted another this year." It was a lie, but by the expression of relief that flickered briefly across Mrs. Cowen's face, Belle knew she did the right thing.

"That's fantastic," Mrs. Cowen said. "I'm so glad you're making friends." *Finally*. She didn't say it, but it was implied. *Finally*, she was recovering from her mother's long drawn out illness and death. *Finally* she was making friends her own age (presumably. Finally, she was *moving on*.

If only it were true. Belle sighed and shook her shoulders in an effort to break free from the gloom that plagued her. Christmas was supposed to be the happiest time of the year, but for her the opposite was true.

She donned her reading glasses and got to work. Nothing like losing oneself in a mass of accounting numbers to forget ones problems.

The bell tinkled above the door, and a blast of cold air came in with a customer. Belle glanced up over her glasses. Standing inside the shop was a man, about her age, mid-twenties or so, dressed in army fatigues. He removed his hat when he saw her. She slipped off her glasses.

Air escaped her lungs and her jaw went slack. He was very good-looking—what girl didn't love a man in uniform? His hair was buzzed short, blond with a hint of red, his face shaved clean, and he had a firm jaw and straight nose. His skin was ruddy with a smattering of freckles. His eyes were dark in the light of the shop and they crinkled at the corners when he smiled. At her. Belle's heart flittered around like a bird wanting out of a cage. She pushed her short, dark hair behind her ears in a nervous response.

"Can I help you?" she squeaked out.

The soldier ducked his chin as he shook his head. "Just looking."

Belle was grateful she didn't have to stand or walk about the shop for the soldier because quite honestly, she didn't trust her knees at this point. Her joints felt like pools of water.

She put her glasses back on and pretended to busy herself, but who was she kidding? How could she concentrate on bookwork with a guy like *him* in the shop? Her eyes darted repeatedly to the soldier. She was careful that he didn't catch her staring.

Until he did. He glanced up from the book in his hand to where she sat behind the counter and then away again. They played that game for several minutes until a chuckle escaped her lips, and she slapped a hand over her mouth.

The soldier selected a book and approached her. Belle removed her glasses and wiped damp palms off on her black trousers.

He slid a gently used version of Stephan Lawhead's book, *The Paradise War*–first book in the *Song of Albion Trilogy*, across the counter.

"Nice choice," she said.

"Thanks." The soldier stared at her name tag, then added, "Belle Vaughn."

Belle rang up his order and the soldier handed her a five-pound note. "I'm Lieutenant Ian Connor, by the way. Since I know your name, I thought it only fair to tell you mine."

"I appreciate the equal opportunity," Belle said with a grin. She motioned to his uniform "Are you recently back or on your way out?"

"I'm on leave for a month."

"Nice for you to be home for the holidays." She slipped his purchase into a bag and handed it to him.

Ian smiled. "It sure is." He tucked the bag under his arm. "Thanks."

Just as he grabbed the doorknob, Belle blurted, "Thanks for shopping at King's Books. We hope to see you again!"

Oh, God. Her face burned with embarrassment. Why did she feel compelled to yell out that dumb, rote response? Mrs. Cowen had drilled it into her, but there was a time and a season for everything (a quote from her mother, God rest her soul) and this was not the time or the season for *that*.

Ian eyes narrowed quizzically. "I hope so, too."

Belle wiggled her fingers. "Bye, Lieutenant Connor."

The soldier disappeared out the door and Belle slumped into her chair with a groan. No wonder she was still single.

About the Author

Lee Strauss is the author of the Minstrel Series (contemporary romance), the Perception Series (young adult dystopian) and young adult historical fiction. She also writes younger YA fantasy as Elle Strauss.

To hear about new releases and promotions sign up for Lee's newsletter at **leestraussbooks.com.**

If you enjoyed reading *Heart & Soul*, please consider leaving a review. Reviews are very helpful to Indie authors and help readers discover the books they love.

ACKNOWLEDGEMENTS

Thanks again and again to my beta readers, Angelika, Juanita and Denise and to Debbie Moore for checking that my use of British lingo sounds authentic; my online writing community without whom I'd be toast in a major way including The Indelibles, Dauntless Authors, Club Indie and my Street Team; my editor Marie Jaskulka, my cover designer Steven Novak and my formatter Ali Cross; the musical artists who believe in trying new colaborations, Tasia Strauss, Andrew Smith, Norm Strauss and Joshua Smith; my husband and musician/music producer, Norm Strauss whose talent and proximity to me continue to make The Minstrel Series possible; to the Donna Petch, Shawn Giesbrecht and Norine Stewart for your ongoing prayer and support, to my parents for holding down the Canadian fort, my kids for being just plain awesome, and to God who carries me through all things.being just plain awesome, and to God who carries me through all things.

SONGS

Summertime (remake) Tasia Straus
Holes in the Night Sky (remake) Tasia Strauss
Holes in the Night Sky (original) by Andrew Smith
Lift Me High (remake) Tasia Strauss

Listen to all the songs from The Minstrel Series on Bandcamp at www.songsfromtheminstrel.bandcamp.com

Scan the QR code to hear the songs featured in *Heart & Soul*

Want more info and features about The Minstrel Series? Visit TheMinstrelSeries.blogspot.com.

ARTIST LINKS

Andrew Smith
andrewsmithmusic.com

Norm Strauss
normstrauss.com

Joel Strauss
joelstrauss.com
joelstrauss.bandcamp.com

Joshua Smith
joshuasmithtunes.com
joshuasmith.bandcamp.com

The Perception Trilogy
Ambition (short story prequel)
Perception (book 1)
Volition (book 2)
Contrition (book 3)

Jars of Clay (vol. 1)
Broken Vessels (vol. 2)

Playing with Matches
A Piece of Blue String
(companion story to *Playing with Matches*)

Contemporary Romance
East of the Sun

The Minstrel Series
Sun & Moon
Flesh & Bone
Heart & Soul
Peace & Goodwill (~ a Christmas novella)

Mystery Suspense
A Nursery Rhyme Suspense
Run, Run, Run (Episode 1/ Part1)

Don't miss out on news of new releases and promotions, sign up for my newsletter **leestraussbooks.com**.

Made in the USA
Charleston, SC
15 November 2014